First published in 2017 in Great Britain by
Barrington Stoke Ltd
18 Walker Street, Edinburgh, EH3 7LP

www.barringtonstoke.co.uk

A CIP catalogue record for this book is available
from the British Library upon request

ISBN: 978-1-78112-728-5

Printed in China by Leo

the last days of archie maxwell

Annabel Pitcher

Barrington Stoke

For my sons, Isaac and Sebastian

"So, that's what we've decided. It's for the best,"
Dad said, after two or ten minutes of talking, Archie
couldn't tell. Time was standing still, or going fast,
or doing both. That wasn't possible, but Dad's words
hadn't seemed possible that morning, and yet here
they were, discussing divorce over Mum's homemade
chicken stew.

Not that anybody was eating the stew. Five plates
cooled on the kitchen table. Their dog, Huxley, sniffed
the chickeny air and let out a whimper. It was a
desolate sound. Archie felt it in his bones.

Archie buried his bare feet in Huxley's thick fur
and glanced at Maisy. Her face was unreadable.
Anything could have been happening beneath the
layers of brown stuff covering her spots. The false
eyebrows she'd painted half way up her forehead
made her seem startled, like this was as big a shock to

her as it was to Archie, but he couldn't be sure. Her real eyebrows might have looked less surprised.

Amy's expression was the opposite, heartbreak written all over her face. Archie never touched his sisters if he could help it, but today he squeezed Amy's pudgy knee. She looked surprised then grabbed Archie's hand with both of hers and didn't let go.

Dad cleared his throat.

"What I mean is – that's what *I've* decided. It's my fault, for reasons that … Well, we'll come to." Dad swallowed. "The important thing is to be good for Mum. This isn't her fault. Do you understand? I take full responsibility."

Dad didn't sound like himself. He didn't look like himself, either. On a normal Friday, he'd have changed out of his work clothes the second he got home, but today he had a job to do, and he was wearing his suit to prove it. Dad's coat looked ominous, hanging on the back of his chair, rather than in the cupboard under the stairs. His bunch of keys was a silver spider next to his plate. Poised. Ready to dart off into the night. Archie downed his water, imagining trapping the spider beneath his glass.

"No, Tim," Mum said. "It's nobody's fault. Not really." It was the first time she'd spoken since Dad had broken the news, and she sounded calmer than Archie had expected. A flicker of irritation licked his insides. Why wasn't Mum crying? Or Dad, for that matter? This was an emergency, wasn't it? A disaster? They should have been frantic, out of control.

But Dad was smiling. "Thanks, Jo. Honestly. I appreciate you saying that, especially in front of the kids."

"Well," Mum said. "There's no point in pretending, is there? The writing's been on the wall for so long."

Archie wondered why they weren't trying to scribble that writing out. He looked around for a pen. He wanted to scrawl a new message on that bastard wall that said something about *love* and something about *forever* and something about *staying together for the sake of the children.*

3

That's how Archie felt – like a small, frightened child. He was glad of Amy's hand in his.

"It's sad," Mum said. "But there you are."

She let out a long sigh, and then there was silence, broken only by Huxley, whining softly as the stew went cold.

The clocks had gone back the day before, and the kitchen seemed too dark for teatime. Mum and Dad's words hung in the gloom. Mum and Dad's words *were* the gloom.

It was unbearable. Archie stood up.

"Are you OK, love?" Mum asked.

Outside, a train chugged along the track at the bottom of the garden, dimly lit carriages skimming the black hedge. The train was there and then it was gone, and Archie wished he could jump on board and disappear too.

"Love, are you all right?" Mum said again.

Archie flicked a switch and sat back down. The kitchen filled with light, but it wasn't enough. He needed candles and the Christmas fairy lights from the loft and Dad's head torch from the box of hiking stuff in the garage. They'd wild camped in the Lake District last year, just him and Dad, trekking up a mountain and putting up a two-man tent on the bank of a river. They were the only ones there, the only ones in the world. They'd played endless games of rummy by the light of the head torch. Pissed behind a rock beneath the moon.

"Shit! Shit ... freezing my bollocks off!" Dad had cried as he'd peed, and Archie had almost died from laughing.

"Me too!" Archie had said, and then, after a pause, "Shit!"

Archie had waited for a telling-off that hadn't come. Dad had simply done up his fly then opened his rucksack, pulling out a tin of beans. They'd cooked the beans on a camping stove, dunking bread because they hadn't got spoons, and then they'd stood on stepping stones in the middle of the river, howling like wolves at the moon. Archie had never felt so strong or powerful or wild, his hair swept back by the wind.

He wanted to lasso that moon and haul it out of the past and into his kitchen to banish the darkness.

"It's for the best," Dad said for the second time that evening.

The flicker of irritation became an inferno in Archie's gut. He burned with it, red-hot. Archie freed himself from Amy's grasp and pressed his palms against the cool table. His arms jerked as he pictured pushing it over, plates smashing and Mum's stew splattering the floor.

Archie dared himself to do it, counting slowly, his fingers pulsating with the need to do something – anything – to shut Dad up. *One ... two ... three ...*

"People break up all the time," Dad said.

Four ... Five ...

"Not for this reason, necessarily, which we ... which *I* will come to. Soon enough."

Six ... Seven ...

"But it's normal, isn't it?" Dad went on. "Splitting up?"

Eight ... Nine ...

Mum nodded too hard. "In some ways it's boringly predictable."

TEN.

Archie willed his hands to move, but nothing happened. A volcano erupted soundlessly in his stomach.

"I know it's a lot to take on board," Mum said, "but it really is for the best." She smiled at Archie and his sisters. Her attempt at warmth was met with ice. Mum's eyes filled with tears, and Archie wondered how long she'd been holding them back. "Look. I get it, OK. I know you're upset. I am too. Your dad and I ... We're both gutted. Gutted to have to break this news. This isn't easy for us. Not by a long stretch. It's just ... some things can't be helped, you know? No matter how much you wish they were different."

Dad leaned forward so far his tie almost dipped in the cold stew on his plate. "I've spent a long time wishing I was different. Trust me. Almost every day of my adult life."

Mum touched Dad's hand. "Oh, Tim."

Archie frowned. It made no sense. When Leon's

parents split up, his mum threw things at a wall and his dad hacked up her favourite dress with the kitchen scissors. And yet here Archie's parents were, sitting at the same table in front of a homemade tea, squeezing each other's fingers.

"The important thing is, we're still good friends," Mum said. "We've always been good friends." For some reason, she shook her head at this. "Maybe that's the problem. We've only ever been –"

"Let's leave it there for now," Dad interrupted. "There's no rush."

Mum nodded. Something silent passed between them, right in front of Archie, but unknowable.

"What you need to understand is that we love you," Dad said. "Very much. And that won't change no matter where I live."

"Where are you going, Daddy?" Amy asked in a tiny voice. Her hands were fists, balled up in her lap.

"Just to a friend's," Dad replied, too quickly. He scratched the side of his head. "Down in Kirkburton. Not far."

"This friend of yours," Maisy said, her tone hinting at something Archie didn't understand. "What's he called?"

There was the longest pause. "Malcolm."

Dad stared at Maisy and she stared back. Archie drifted out of the window and floated in the black beyond the glass.

"This is bull," Maisy said. "Bull!" She stood up so suddenly, her chair flew back and clattered to the floor. "Malcolm? Really? Is this a frickin' joke?"

"Language, Maisy!" Mum said. She put her hands over Amy's ears, but Amy squirmed free.

"I'm not six!"

"No, you're seven. Too young to –"

"*Frickin'* is not a fucking swear word," Maisy said before storming out of the kitchen.

"Get back here!" Mum called as the door slammed and Amy burst into tears. "Now look! You've upset your sister!"

"*Maisy* didn't upset me," Amy said. "You did!" And then she ran off too.

Archie remained at the table. Mum seemed to be holding her breath. Archie wanted to shout, to kick over his chair, to fling open the back door and flounce off into the night, but Mum's blue eyes were pools of sadness and Dad was patting him on the back.

"Women, eh?" Dad said.

"Boys are so much easier than girls. I've said it a million times." Mum reached across the table and touched the pale scar that ran down Archie's cheek. "Apart from the silly cuts and bruises, but I'd take those any day." She clutched Archie's hand, rubbing his knuckles with her thumb. "You're a good boy, Arch. Always have been. And it will be OK. I promise."

Archie wanted to believe her. He longed to feel the flutter of hope in his chest, but his heart had lost its wings. Time was slowing down now, no doubt about it. The volcano had subsided. There was only ash. Smoke. Darkness.

"Eat your tea, love," Mum said.

Archie did as he was told.

2

Archie trudged upstairs to find Maisy in the bathroom, bent over the sink, splashing her face with water.

"You OK?" he asked. Maisy looked at him then splashed her face some more. Archie could tell she'd been crying. He wished he could cry. His tears felt far away, deep underground, trapped beneath something cold and hard.

"That was, er, that was ... Wasn't it?" Archie said. He hovered by the door, unsure whether he was allowed to enter. Maisy turned off the tap and stared in the mirror, blanking him completely. "Can I come in?"

Maisy didn't reply. Her make-up was gone, apart from two dark smudges under her eyes – blue eyes, like Mum and Amy, not hazel ones, like him and Dad. Maisy's spots were more visible now, but Archie thought she looked nicer with her face uncovered.

Softer. She frowned with her real eyebrows, these faint, fuzzy things.

"Are you OK?" Archie repeated, and this time he entered the bathroom.

"Oh, I'm fabulous." Maisy dried her face then shoved the towel on the radiator. "Bloody brilliant."

Archie closed the toilet lid and perched on it, taking one of Dad's puzzle books from the shelf behind the loo. He glanced at a couple of pages then threw the book to one side. "Yeah," Archie said. "Same here."

Maisy plonked down by the radiator and kicked out her legs. "I just don't get it. I really don't." She picked some skin off the side of her thumb nail then tossed it away. "I mean, I've known. Sort of. Guessed it, you know? There were some pretty big clues."

"Yeah, there were," Archie said, even though he had no idea what Maisy was talking about.

Maisy went at another bit of skin, this time on her little finger, tearing at it with her nails before biting it and spitting it away. "Malcolm!"

"I don't know him," Archie said. "Do you?"

Maisy let out an odd bark of laughter. "Dad's not exactly going to parade him in front of us, is he? Of course we don't know him."

"Suppose," Archie replied, but he was bluffing. If Malcolm was a close enough friend to invite Dad to stay at his house for a few days, Archie thought there was a good chance he might have heard of him before.

"What do you think Malcolm looks like?" Maisy asked.

Archie hesitated. "What's it matter?"

"In my head, he's a bit like Graham Norton," Maisy went on. "But younger. I've got this horrid feeling that he's about nineteen and they met online."

Archie wrinkled his nose. "Nah. Dad hates all that stuff. He's always on at us to live in the *real* world."

"Where else could they have met?"

"Anywhere. At work. The football. Or he might be one of Dad's old school friends."

Maisy drew up her knees to her chest and rested her chin in the groove. "Online. Trust me. I just don't think it's that easy in real life. Not if you're married. How do you even have the conversation?"

Archie wanted to ask what type of conversation she meant, but he was afraid of sounding stupid. "I think he's met someone," he said, to prove he wasn't totally naïve. "I reckon he's been having an affair."

Maisy looked at him sideways without moving her head. "What?"

"An affair," Archie said. "Don't you think? That's what happened to Leon. His mum was screwing the man who walked their dog. *Happy Hound –*"

"I bet he was."

"No, that's the name of the company. *Happy Hound Dog –*"

"I know, Archie."

"Well, there you go. Maybe Dad's met someone too."

Maisy lifted her head. "You are kidding, right?"

Archie paused. He didn't want to hurt Maisy, but it felt good to be a couple of steps ahead for once. "I just think someone else is involved. That's why he was

14

scared of telling us the real reason he was leaving. He
didn't want to say in front of Amy."

Maisy rested her head back on the radiator and
closed her eyes. "Oh, Archie."

"I'm sorry," Archie said. "I might be wrong, but –"

"He *has* met someone, you idiot."

"What? How do you know? What's her name?"

It took for ever, but at last Maisy opened one eye.
"*His* name, Archie. His name is Malcolm."

$$|\,|\,|$$

"Are you ready?" Dad called up the stairs the next day.
"Archie?"

Archie was ready, dressed in his football kit, but
he didn't move from his bedroom window.

The sun was angry that morning, a fiery ball
raging against the sky, and Archie wanted to feel its
fury. But there was nothing. He watched the red fade
to white and the world bleach of colour, his heart
beating out the endless seconds against his ribs.

Grandpa used to say something about a shepherd and a red sky. Archie tried to remember the rhyme, but his brain was slow and foggy, full of the mist that had now settled on the track at the end of the garden.

"Get a move on, Arch!" Dad called a few minutes later. "We've got to go!"

Even if he'd wanted to move, Archie didn't think he could have walked downstairs. He wasn't entirely sure he still had legs. He supposed the feet on the carpet must belong to him, but there was no feeling at all in his toes.

Toes were strange.

And ankles, now he looked at them – two bumps jutting out like knobbly, prehistoric skulls. He yawned, feeling 150,000 years old. He hadn't slept at all, just stared at the black ceiling for hours trying to forget Maisy's words because they were complete and utter –

"Horse shit," Archie said out loud. "Total balls."

His protest fogged up the window. He was ashamed of it. He had no problem with men like Graham Norton.

He just didn't want his dad to become one of them. With the sleeve of his hoody, Archie made a hole in the fog and gazed at the rectangle of lawn where he'd learned to play football, scoring goals and running around the garden with his hands in the air. Dad had done the same, making crazy laps in the opposite direction. Every time they'd passed, they'd given each other a high five that got higher and higher and wilder and wilder, Dad holding his hand just out of arm's reach so Archie had to jump. They were Chelsea. Bayern Munich. Real Madrid. World beaters. Champions. Archie had believed they were capable of anything.

His door opened, but Archie didn't turn around.

"Come on," Dad said. "We should have left ten minutes ago."

Archie couldn't bring himself to meet Dad's eyes – hazel eyes, like Archie's, though he wasn't even sure of this anymore. In fact, now Archie tried, he couldn't picture Dad's face. There was just a blur, a question mark hovering over Dad's head like a peculiar halo, shrouding him in mystery.

"Have you got everything you need?" Dad asked.

Outside, a train appeared from the mist, heading to Huddersfield, just like it did at twenty-nine minutes past every hour from dawn until dusk. Archie wanted to smash his window and leap onto the train with its fixed, steady wheels and reliable timetable. He'd sit on it all day, chugging up and down the track, knowing exactly what was coming at any given moment.

"Arch?" said Dad. "Don't ignore me, son."

Even Dad's voice sounded strange. Was it Archie's imagination, or did it seem a little more high-pitched than normal? Was this one of the clues that Maisy had meant? If Archie sneaked a look at Dad, would it be obvious?

No.

NO.

He knew Dad. And he knew he wasn't –

He knew he wasn't –

He knew that Maisy was wrong.

Archie steeled himself and turned around. Dad's eyes were hazel. He was dressed in the tracksuit top he always wore to watch Archie play football. All was as it should be, and Archie's legs came back to him in a wobble of relief.

"Good lad. Mum said you might not feel like it today, but I knew you'd want to play." Dad gestured to the badge on Archie's shirt. "Not let the team down, eh? That's my boy. Carry on as normal, that's what we'll do. Every Saturday, I'll pick you up and off we'll go, right? It'll be just the same." Dad walked over and grabbed Archie's shoulder, squeezing too hard. "We've always been good pals, you and me. That's not going to change. I'll always be your dad, no matter what happens. No matter where I live."

"When?" Archie asked. "When are you going to move in with –"

Dad blushed, even though no name had been mentioned. Archie didn't like the look of all that red. It hinted at something dangerous, and Grandpa's rhyme came back to Archie in a whisper, and then a shout.

Red in the morning, shepherd's warning.

"Next week," Dad said, at last. "When I've got myself sorted."

"But just for a few days," Archie replied. "And then you'll find your own place."

It wasn't a question so Dad didn't answer. "Got your boots? Right. Let's go."

3

"Trust me, she'll be gagging for it," Leon said during break on Monday as Archie stood by the picnic benches with the boys he still found it hard to believe were actually his mates. He had Leon to thank for this crowd. Their mums had been friends for decades, so when Archie moved schools last year, Leon took him under his wing. It wasn't always a comfortable place to be, but it was better than being alone. The loner in the dining hall. The loser killing time in the library. At his old school, Archie had been on top of all his homework. Now, he was always behind.

Leon did something filthy with a Twix that made Jack and Mo laugh. Archie joined in a second too late, the sound rattling around his skull.

"Tia would love a bit of that," Leon said. "Grief makes you horny. I read it."

Mo emptied a packet of Skittles into his hand. "Where?"

"I dunno. Online somewhere. What's it matter? I said I read it, so I read it." Leon took a bite of the Twix and chewed slowly. "Lots of people get their end away after a funeral. Grief makes girls wet. And vulnerable." He smirked. "Look at her, cocks. She's a mess."

Archie glanced at Tia. It wasn't easy. He had to will his eyes to move, and even then he couldn't look at her directly. She was dazzling, even as she hunched over a picnic table, sobbing into a tissue. Her best friend, Jared, was patting her on the back, but it didn't seem to be helping.

"Bit late to be pissing and moaning about it now," Jack said, through a mouthful of pickled onion Monster Munch. "It was ages ago, wasn't it?"

Leon made a show of gagging. "Those things fucking stink. Stand over there."

"Yeah, but why cry about it now?" Jack asked, moving to the spot Leon had pointed out. "Wasn't it last year?"

Leon tossed the Twix wrapper on the ground even though he was standing next to a bin. "A year ago this week." He smirked again. "The gift that keeps on giving. Praise the Lord that stupid prick jumped."

Archie would have winced if he hadn't trained his face to stay neutral, but Tia didn't seem to have heard. She breathed in deeply, using the base of her palms to wipe her face before arching her back in a cat-like stretch. It was too much. She was too much. She was everything.

Archie shoved his hands in his pockets and counted down from ten to one. It didn't work. All the benches were full, so he sat down on a patch of grass in front of the P.E. block and put his rucksack on his knees, trying to look relaxed as he waited for The Tia Effect to subside. That's what he secretly called it whenever this happened. He rummaged about in his bag then took out a bottle of Coke, making a big deal of having a sip.

Leon threw Archie a glance, his black eyes hard as rocks. "Where do you think you are, at the fucking seaside?"

Archie didn't stand up. He couldn't. The Tia Effect was particularly strong today.

"Nah, just knackered, mate," Archie replied, which was true. The bags beneath his eyes were big enough to suffocate in. He imagined pulling out the purple skin and wrapping it around his head so that he couldn't breathe. His lungs would tingle and then burn and then ... what? What happened when the fire went out?

Tia's brother, Tathum, had been curious too. And then Tathum had found out, discovering the truth almost twelve months ago as he jumped in front of the Huddersfield train, less than fifty metres from the end of Archie's back garden. It was a school day so Archie missed the drama. By the time he got home, trains were moving up and down the track as if nothing at all had happened.

But then, the very next day, flowers had appeared, hundreds of white roses in a pristine carpet on the muddy embankment that Archie could see from his bedroom window. He'd watched, pulse racing, as Tia visited the track – this girl from his new school who he'd spotted in the first week and had liked ever since. She'd stood among the flowers, which seemed to bob and sway, though the morning was still. It was a magic carpet, hovering above the track, and Tia had flown to Archie, surrounded by petals, and he'd leaped from his window into her outstretched arms, kissing her in a way that made the white flowers blush.

Archie had felt guilty for thinking such things when Tia was suffering, and even worse for doing what he needed to do when these thoughts crossed his mind. It had been risky, because she could have squinted up at his window at any moment. That made it better and worse, and harder and easier, and his heart was pounding and his wrist was aching, and then it was over, and Archie could look at Tia, wrapped up in her black coat, without wondering what it would be like to take it off.

Down by the track, Tia had glanced over her shoulder – once, twice – before laying a single red rose and hurrying away. It was the only speck of colour on the carpet of white. White for Yorkshire. White for

Leeds United, Tia's brother's favourite team. He'd had trials for the under-16s just two weeks before he died, or so the papers said beneath headlines that claimed his death was "A Baffling Mystery", "A Senseless Suicide", "A Tragic Waste".

But what did the red stand for?

When Archie had checked the rose a little later, climbing over the wall at the end of his garden and creeping along the sloped embankment, he wasn't surprised to find that it had no note. The rose spoke of something too profound – or secret – for words. The petals were the colour of blood. Of flesh. Part of Tia's heart had been placed by the track. Sometimes, when he drifted off to sleep, Archie could still hear it beating ...

Leon nudged Archie with his foot, and then again, harder, kicking him on the shin. "Oi, space cadet! You got a ball?"

Archie always had a ball. He took it out of his bag and threw it up at Leon, who headed it in Tia's direction.

"Here we go, cocks," Leon said. "Wish me luck."

|||

The ball rolled below Tia's picnic table. Leon followed.
It irritated Archie and, as much as he hated to admit
it, impressed him too. Archie could never do that. He
could never *walk* like that, with an easy swagger, as if
he had all the time in the world. Nothing was rushed,
nothing was forced, because everything would unfold
exactly as Leon planned. It always did.

"Can I get the ball?"

"Yeah, sure," Tia said, but Leon was already stooping
under the table. The ball was by her feet. Archie bit his
cheek as Leon's hand edged closer to Tia's pink laces.

Most boys banged on about Tia's boobs and
bum. But for Archie it was those laces, never tied
neatly, always trailing from her black Converse. It
drove him crazy, wondering why a girl with perfect
hair and make-up had laces like that. They hinted
at something real, something wonderful. A messy
bedroom. Eating ham straight from the packet in the
fridge. Slugging milk from the bottle when no one else

was around. The laces seemed to suggest that she'd be up for watching *Match of the Day* in one of Archie's old T-shirts, cuddled up in his bed with Huxley farting away on the floor. *I accept you* – that's what the laces told him. *I accept you, just as you are ...*

Even if your dad turns out to be ...

Even if your dad turns out to be ...

Even if your dad turns out to be ...

Gay.

This was the first time Archie had let himself say that word, even inside his head.

Gay. GAY. Dad was –

"Such a bender," Mo said, and Archie was so surprised he dropped the Coke bottle. Mo had heard. Somehow he had heard, or sensed the truth, and now the secret was out. Coke fizzed everywhere, brown liquid sloshing over the grass as Archie looked up, half-expecting to see the word scrawled across the sky. The sun was a spotlight, singling him out. It was a projector, shining his innermost secrets onto the grey wall of the P.E. block.

Archie turned around sharply, but there was nothing, just concrete and windows and Mr Owen sipping coffee and checking his watch, because Archie's life was surely about to end.

"So frickin' bent," Mo said. "Look at him."

Mo was eyeballing someone. Archie followed his gaze.

Jared.

Archie picked up the bottle and gulped down the last of the Coke.

"Why does Tia hang around with such a poof?" Mo asked as Jared tested Tia's bronze eyeshadow on the back of his hand, holding it up to the sun to make it sparkle.

Archie's tongue felt too big for his mouth. "No idea, mate. But he seems all right."

Mo's head jerked back in surprise. "You serious? He likes boys."

Archie attempted a shrug, but the weight of the world was on his shoulders. "I'm just saying, he seems all right."

Mo spat on the ground, but said nothing more.

"Do you think he's forgotten that's my ball?"
Archie asked to change the subject. It was tucked
under Leon's arm as he chatted to Tia, trying to make
her laugh. It worked, her face breaking into a smile
that showed every one of her straight, white teeth.

Leon grinned. "I knew I could cheer you up. Mind
if I sit?" He didn't wait for a reply, straddling the
bench and moving in close.

Jared shoved a few things into a silver rucksack.
"Well, I know where I'm not wanted."

"Hey, you don't have to go!" Tia said, making a
grab for Jared's hand.

"It's OK. Roles reversed, I'd tell you to piss off."
Jared winked at Tia and then left, walking straight
past Archie, the sun bouncing off his silver rucksack.

"See what I mean?" Mo muttered, pointing at the
rainbow on Jared's bag. "That's the gay flag, right?
It's like he's proud of it."

Archie didn't reply. He watched Jared stroll
across the playground, not a care in the world, which

was how it should be. Archie knew that. But it was different with Dad. Dad had a normal, non-silvery rucksack, one with a built-in water pouch that he took hiking. That's who Dad was, who he'd been for forty-three years. He couldn't suddenly start wearing a rainbow rucksack and expect no one to mind.

Jack appeared at Archie's side, smelling of pickled onion Monster Munch. "Look at you, perving at the poof."

"Shut up, man," Archie replied. "I'm not perving."

"Don't diss the poof," Mo said. "Archie loves the poof. Even though he wears make-up like a girl."

"That's not what I said."

Mo pretended to think. "What was it again? *He's a bit of all right?*"

"Don't be a dick," Archie said. "He's *all right*. That's what I said. He's all right."

"He's all wrong," Jack replied and Mo snorted. "If you can't see that he's a freak, you must be as bent as he is. Queer boy."

Archie's stomach dropped, even though he knew it

wasn't true. It couldn't be true. Could it? He looked the same as Dad – everyone always said so. What if they shared more than just hazel eyes? What if –

"He's not even denying it!" Jack said.

"Because it's true. Have you ever seen Archie with a girl?" Mo asked. "Like, ever in your life?"

Jack's eyes widened as he pointed at Archie's face. "Sara's party."

Archie knew what was coming next. He tried to hit Jack's finger away, but Jack dodged him and poked him on the cheek, right on his scar. It tingled as some old hurt returned. Two boys from his old school forcing Archie down to the ground ... A boot ... And blood. Archie's heart sped up at the memory, sped up as Jack opened his mouth and said,

"Izzie wanted to get off with you and you said no because you liked someone else, but you wouldn't tell us who. Who does that? Who says no to Izzie Richards? She's –" Jack spread his palms in front of his chest "– *big*."

"It's because he likes Jared!" Mo said. "That's why! He loves The Gay!"

32

Jack raised his hand and Mo met it in a jubilant high-five. The sound was a gun-shot and Archie wished it had actually blown out his brains because this – all of it – was too much to take.

"You do, don't you?" Mo went on. "Admit it, Arch! You may as well."

"Yeah, you got me." It took Archie all his energy, but he shoved Mo playfully and forced a smile. "Knobs."

"You like knobs?" Jack said and Mo roared with laughter.

"One knob in particular! Jared's! Up his arse!" Mo yelled, miming the action, but it was Dad who Archie could see – Dad bending over, Dad with his bum in the air.

"Give up, will you?" Archie said. "It isn't funny."

"It's fucking funny," Jack said, swivelling his hips. "Ooh, check me out. I'm Archie Gaylord."

Mo dropped to his knees. "And I'm his little cock muncher, Jared Queer." He jerked his head back and forth as if sucking, and then he *was* sucking, and Archie's dad was squirming in pleasure.

"Stop it!"

"Hit a nerve, have we?"

"I'm serious. Just stop it, all right?" Archie closed his eyes, but it was no good. Malcolm strolled into his mind. "Stop it. Please!"

Malcolm started to undress for Dad, who was already naked and aroused, The Malcolm Effect far bigger than The Tia Effect had ever been. And then Dad and Malcolm started doing things, unspeakable things, their groans blocking out the jeers of Archie's mates, who seemed a million miles away in a different school, in a different land.

Archie had never felt so alone.

There was so much space between him and the rest of the world, a strange sense of unreality washed over him, like a dark sea from another universe. He was drowning in it. Sounds were muffled, his vision blurred.

Archie wouldn't have known it was Tia if it weren't for the hot pink laces.

She was standing in front of him, and because this

was a peculiar planet in an unfamiliar solar system where the normal rules did not apply, she said his name.

"Archie? Can we talk?"

4

The question brought Archie back to his senses. He dropped from outer space and clattered onto the playground a couple of metres from where Tia was standing, her hands tucked deep in the pockets of the black coat. The same coat she was wearing that day at the track.

Archie couldn't look at it. He couldn't look at her.

Tia had left Leon straddling the picnic bench. He was facing the opposite direction, but Archie could tell he was straining to listen. It was something about Leon's straight back and long neck, the way his head was cocked to one side.

"Archie?" Tia said again, taking a step forward.

It was easier for Archie to look at the sun than it was to meet her gaze. He stared over her shoulder at the hazy circle in the grey sky.

"It is Archie, right? Right?" Tia asked Jack and Mo,

who had frozen on the playground, Mo on all-fours and Jack grasping Mo's hips, mid-thrust. Tia frowned, and Archie suddenly felt less alone. "That's not funny, you know," Tia said.

Mo clambered to his feet and brushed mud off his knees. "Lighten up. We're just joking around."

"Hilarious." Tia rolled her big, brown eyes. "Brilliant. Really witty and intelligent. Well done."

"All right, you sarky bitch," Jack said.

Tia put her hand on her chest, as if it were a compliment. "Your mum must be so proud."

"Think you're funny?" Mo said. "Sarcasm is the –"

"Lowest form of wit. Yeah, I know. But at least it's *a* form of wit, unlike –" Tia waved her hand vaguely "– I don't even know what to call it – your general dickheadedness."

"Fuckwittedness," Archie said, just loud enough for Tia to hear. "Dickheadedness is too polite."

Tia didn't smile, but that little nod was enough. Somehow, right now, they were on the same team. "Can we talk?" she said.

"To him?" came a voice. "Really?" Leon was hurrying so quickly across the playground, he seemed to have left his swagger behind. "Archie?"

"Yeah," Tia said. "Why not?"

"Because he's – well, *Archie*."

"Anyway, you can't," Jack said, grabbing the ball off Leon. "He's got a job to do." Jack booted the ball as hard as he could. Everyone watched it soar over the wire mesh fence and bounce onto the playing field. "See? He needs to go and get it before the bell goes in, *ooh* –" Jack checked his phone "– about thirty-seven seconds."

Leon laughed, but unusually for him, it sounded forced.

"Pathetic," Tia said. "But, whatever. I'll keep Archie company. If that's OK?"

She turned to Archie, her face a question, which was crazy, because surely she knew – surely it was obvious – that the answer to anything she ever asked of him would always be *yes*. Archie's entire body screamed it so loudly he didn't have to speak.

"Great." Tia smiled then, just a little bit. "Let's go."

||||

The bell rang. Archie and Tia checked that Mr Owen was distracted, and then made a dash for it. No one saw. No one shouted them back. They were free. They passed through a gap in the fence as if stepping into a different world, sharing a glance as they half ran down the slope, trying not to lose their footing.

The field stretched out before them. They were alone. Anything could happen, anything at all, but Archie couldn't think about that and keep a clear head, so he jogged up to the ball, did a neat step-over and flicked it high into the air.

"You're good," Tia said. The ball dropped and Archie smashed it into the top left corner of the goal. "Nice."

Archie grinned. "Cheers. What lesson are you missing?"

"Maths. Mr Raj. I'll say I had to go to Sick Bay for female reasons," Tia said, opening a packet of mints. "Mr Raj won't argue with that."

"Cool," Archie said, though he was anything but, his cheeks pink at the mention of something so intimate. "Yeah, I'll do the same." Tia raised an eyebrow. "Not ... *the same, the same* obviously. I won't go for a female reason. I'll go for a male reason."

"What type of male reason?" There was a hint of a giggle in Tia's voice.

The tips of Archie's ears were sizzling now. "Unisex then. A unisex reason. I dunno. A headache."

"A headache's too predictable. Go for something different. Neck ache. Indigestion. Maybe you ate one too many of these," Tia said, stepping closer to offer him a mint. She smiled as Archie took one, her teeth white and straight except for a tiny overlap in the two at the front. Archie had never noticed it before. Tia touched her mouth. "Have I got food in my teeth?"

"No, they're –" He was going to say *perfect*, but lost his nerve at the last moment – "very clean."

Archie cringed, but Tia seemed amused. "Good to know." She flopped back on the grass and closed her eyes. Archie did the same, though his eyelids kept fluttering apart to make quite sure he wasn't dreaming.

"So, this is awesome," Tia said, and Archie put his hands behind his head and basked in her words as if they were the most perfect summer's day. "Everyone else, stuck indoors. Us out here, not giving a crap. This is fuckin' da man, right?"

Archie snorted. "What the hell was that?"

Tia kicked his foot but didn't open her eyes. "It's something Tathum used to say. My brother. *Fuck da man.* It doesn't sound right when I say it."

"Who's the man?"

Tia giggled, her eyes still shut. "I don't really know. Teachers, I guess?" She waved her hand, her fingers tracing a delicate pattern in the air. "Police? Anyone in charge. The rules, maybe?"

"Which rules?" Archie asked, to keep her talking. He loved watching her mouth as it moved. Lips.

Tongue. Teeth. The secret flaw in the two at the front.

Tia sighed, and her breath smelled of mint. "All the rules. Gazillions of them."

"Is that even a number?"

It was Tia's turn to snort. "Probably not. I'm no good at Maths, which is why I should be in there with Mr Raj rather than out here with you. But screw the rules, right? Screw the rules about what we should do, where we should go."

"Who we should be," Archie said, after a pause filled with thoughts of Dad.

Tia nodded. "Especially that one. That's the worst rule of the lot."

"Fuck da man!" Archie declared. "Fuck da fuckin' man."

"A-men brother."

They did a jokey fist-pump and something dislodged in Archie's chest. Dad was still dad. He still loved football. He still wanted to take Archie to his matches and that wouldn't change no matter where

Dad lived, or who he lived with. Archie inhaled, his lungs filling with air and the mint on Tia's breath and the words of their strange prayer. *Fuck da man.* It was going to be OK. It wasn't going to be easy, but it was –

"Archie?" Tia asked.

He'd let himself forget that Tia had come with him to the playing field for her own reasons. It was a shock to find her sitting up and staring at him.

"I have a few questions, if that's all right?" Tia said.

"Depends what you're going to ask me." It was supposed to be a joke, but the atmosphere had shifted and Archie's words fell flat as it started to rain. "What do you want to know?"

"You live by the track, don't you? I saw you there."

Archie's eyes opened in alarm. He forced himself to blink and tried to look calm. "Yeah, why?" He held up his hand to the sky. "It's peeing it down. We should go in."

"I saw you a few times, actually," Tia went on. "My

friend, Laura, lives near you. On Far End Lane?" Tia
pulled an umbrella from her bag but didn't put it up.
"Can you see the track from your bedroom?"

Archie gagged on his mint, wondering if Tia had
spotted him at the window when she'd laid the rose.
What had she seen? Not *that*, surely? Tia was staring
at Archie, waiting for an answer.

He took a deep breath. "Yeah."

She gasped. "Really?"

"Yeah," Archie said again. "Why?"

"I knew your house overlooked the track but I
didn't know your actual room did too. You must look
at it a lot, right?" Tia was excited, talking quickly.
She watched Archie's face, impatient for a response.
"You'd notice someone, if they were there? You'd see
them, wouldn't you?"

"What's this about? And can we walk at the same
time?" Archie stood up, horribly aware of his skinny
ribs as his wet shirt stuck to his skin. "Come on. Let's
go."

Tia didn't move. "I mean, how could you not? How

could you not see someone by the track if they were there?"

"Umbrella?" Archie said.

At last Tia listened, scrambling to her feet and pressing a button so that a perfect arc of red appeared in the sky. They sheltered under it, their breath coming in warm clouds that mingled in the pinkish light.

"So, did you?" Tia asked, agitated now. "I need to know." They were exactly the same height, their noses almost touching. Tia's eyes weren't just brown, Archie saw. There were flecks of gold, streaks of amber – a fire around her pupils, black as coal. "Did you see my brother by the track?"

"When? On the day he –" Archie couldn't finish the sentence, but Tia was shaking her head.

"No, no. Not then. We were at school. I mean before that. Maybe one weekend or night?" Tia's eyes burned with an emotion Archie couldn't identify. He felt the heat of it, though. The intensity. Tia shook his arm. "Come on, Archie! Think! It's important.

Really important. Because if Tathum was there, like if he went down to the track a few times before the day that he –" she had to force out the words "– *killed* himself then it was what he really wanted, right?"

Hope. That was what it was, blazing in her eyes, and Archie couldn't bear to put it out.

"Yeah," he said at last. "I think I did. Yeah, definitely. I saw him." It didn't feel like a lie, more of a kindness, so Archie added, "A couple of times. Sort of pacing up and down."

"When?" Tia asked. "A week before he died? Two weeks?"

"Er, two weeks, I think. That sounds about right."

"Really? You're sure?" Tia said, and Archie nodded. "That's amazing!" She grabbed his hand. "Thank you! I can't tell you how much that helps. I've driven myself mad! Totally mad, thinking maybe Tathum regretted it after he jumped, wondering if there was this moment before the train hit where he was, like, *Shit, I don't want to die.* But this is proof, isn't it? This is proof that he planned it. That he's at peace."

Archie didn't know what to say, but it didn't matter. Tia squeezed his hand then stepped out from under the umbrella. She turned her face up to the rain and breathed – just breathed – as if she hadn't been able to for a very long time.

"Will you show me?" Tia asked. "Where you saw him pacing about? I'd like to see the place. Maybe one night this week?"

She was shivering now, her shirt almost see-through. Archie couldn't focus on anything other than her dark blue bra. "Sure."

"Thank you!" Tia cried and she ran off, zigzagging across the field, swooping madly, flying with her arms outstretched.

Archie tossed the umbrella to one side and joined in, chasing after her. He was seven years old again, looping around the garden after scoring a goal as Dad made circles in the opposite direction. Archie was a champion. A world beater. He had made Tia happy and it was all he could do not to throw back his head and crow at the sky.

"Honestly, Archie!" Tia yelled. "I feel like I could take off!"

"Let's take off then!" Archie grabbed Tia's waist and lifted her high into the air. He started to spin and she laughed, her arms held aloft. They were floating, flying on a magic carpet of white flowers, the petals turning pink because they knew what was going to happen next.

And it did happen – it did happen! – and Archie's heart was a red rose, blooming in his chest.

5

Archie knew something was wrong the second he stepped through the front door, but he couldn't put his finger on what it was. He stood in the living room and waited for it to come to him.

A silver frame was missing from the mantelpiece, the one that contained a photo of Archie and his sisters on Christmas Day. They'd been out for lunch to a posh restaurant. Dad had booked it as a surprise because he was that sort of man, good with birthdays and Valentine's cards and always arriving home with flowers.

"Just because I'm sorry," Dad had said, a couple of weeks earlier, handing Mum a bunch of sunflowers. There'd been no argument, so it had puzzled Archie at the time. Now it made sense. Mum had looked sad as she'd trimmed the stalks, sticking the sunflowers in a green vase, a few petals falling off as if they were weeping.

There were other things missing too. The cycling magazines from the coffee table. Dad's glasses case from the window sill. His slippers with the hole that Huxley had chewed.

Dad had gone.

Archie hurried from the living room. No tracksuit top in the cupboard under the stairs. No driving licence in the messy tray on top of the microwave. No paperwork piled up on the stairs. Archie sprinted up them, two at a time, but there was no escape at the top. Amy was sobbing in her room. Mum was trying to comfort her. *"Don't worry, love. Don't worry. It will be all right. It will. I promise."*

Archie wished he could believe her.

Dad's toothbrush and razor weren't in the bathroom. Archie lowered the toilet lid and flopped down, his legs a little shaky. A lot shaky. Dad's puzzle books had disappeared too. Archie picked up a can of air freshener that was meant to smell like jasmine but smelled more like Dad because he always sprayed too much. He sniffed the nozzle.

"What are you doing?" Mum said, appearing at the door, a pile of soggy tissues in one hand. "That thing could kill you!"

"How?" Archie asked. "Do you inhale it or is it liquid?"

"What sort of question is that?" Mum snatched the can off Archie and put it in the cupboard above the sink. Archie had been able to reach up there for years and Mum seemed to remember that he wasn't a small child anymore and put the can back by the toilet. "Just leave it alone, all right?" Mum said. "Don't you go funny on me." She held up the tissues. "I've got one daughter sobbing on her bedroom floor and another refusing to come home. Budge, will you?"

"Where's Maisy gone?" Archie asked, getting off the toilet so Mum could drop in the tissues.

"God knows." Mum pulled the flush. "She messaged me to say she was staying over at a friend's and not to worry, she just needed space." Mum perched on the end of the bath where Dad's shampoo had lived until that morning. "Space? There's never been more space. The house feels empty."

Archie sat back down on the toilet. "Are you OK?" he muttered, because it was easier than asking for confirmation that Dad had gone for good.

It didn't seem possible. This was his home. It had spaces for all Dad's things, spaces that didn't vanish just because he'd gone. Archie could see a pair of Dad's blue boxer shorts in the washing basket. Would Mum wash them, or was that no longer right? What if Dad needed them? What if they were his favourite pair, his lucky pair, and he wanted them to –

What?

Impress Malcolm?

"I'm OK," Mum replied, as Malcolm slowly pulled down Dad's boxer shorts.

Archie shook his head to get rid of the image, replacing it with Tia's blue bra strap as he relived the kiss.

The clash of their lips.

The taste of her mouth.

The softness of her tongue.

And his favourite bit – how she'd put her hands on his face, cradling it almost, like it was precious.

But then she'd pulled back, and Archie had seen that she was crying.

"Ignore me. I'm a mess this week," she said, but in Dad's voice now, because it was Dad who Archie had been kissing.

Dad with Tia's hair.

Tia with Dad's fuzzy bald patch.

Dad shivering on the pitch dressed in Tia's blue bra and his matching blue boxer shorts.

"How about you?" Mum asked Archie. "Are you OK?"

"Fine," he said.

"Good." Mum ruffled his hair. "That's all that matters to me, love."

"The house feels weird."

"It's going to be strange at first. It will take some getting used to. No more bits of stubble in there," Mum said, pointing at the sink. "But you'll start leaving them soon!" She ran her thumb across Archie's top lip. "Look! You're getting a bit of a moustache, my boy."

Archie shrugged off her hand. "Mum!"

"I'll get you a razor. Don't want you nicking mine. Or Dad will. He might like to do it. I'll ask him."

"How?" said Archie. "He's not here."

"He's ten minutes away, Arch. Kirkburton, not Timbuktu."

Archie fiddled with the loo roll, tearing off tissue and screwing it up into a ball. "He didn't even say goodbye."

"Because it's not goodbye, love. We thought it would be better for him to move out his stuff while you were at school, that's all. Not make a big scene. Not have everyone sobbing."

"*Yeah, that worked*," Archie wanted to say because Amy was starting up again, howling in her room. Instead, he nodded. "I guess."

Mum moved to the door, distracted by Amy. "It isn't goodbye. He's still welcome here. Any time he likes. He's coming over for tea tonight, in fact. He needs to talk to you all."

Round and round went the ball of tissue between Archie's thumb and finger. Round and round, getting smaller and smaller, as the world closed in.

"I'm doing bangers and mash!" Mum said in a sing-song voice that was clearly meant to raise a smile. "I might even do onion gravy."

Archie didn't give a shit what sort of gravy she made.

He bashed the loo roll, causing it to unwind. Reams of white paper flowed over the floor. He wished Mum would bash his head like that, forcing his brain to spool out of his skull so that his thoughts were visible, the question he was too afraid to ask all too blatant as it clattered onto the tiles.

"Don't do that, Archie. That's just silly." Mum walked over to the loo roll and took it off the holder, winding it up tight. "Listen, I'll tell you what I've told Amy, OK? This isn't the end. Not at all. You'll still see Dad. Every day, if you want to. Dad wants to be

involved as much as ever. You know what he's like.
He's not going to vanish just because –"

"He's gay," Archie said, before he could stop
himself.

Mum's silence told Archie everything he needed
to know. The world shrunk to the size of that word –
just three small letters. There was nothing else. Mum
offered no alternative. Archie pulled at his school tie,
unable to breathe.

"Dad will talk to you tonight," Mum said at last.
"He can explain … Where are you going?"

"Out." Archie had already left the bathroom. He
was in his room, searching for a dog lead in the mess
on his desk, kicking at the clothes on his floor. He
found a lead in the pocket of a coat half-shoved under
his bed.

"No, you're not," Mum said as Archie put on the
coat. He wrapped the lead around his hand until it
hurt. "It's homework time."

Archie frowned. "Maisy's out."

"Yes, and I've texted her to tell her to come home."

"Please, Mum. Just for a bit." Archie looked at her, really looked at her for the first time since Friday, shocked by the greyness of her skin, the deepness of the frown lines. He wondered if his face had changed too – it seemed impossible that he could still be the same person. "I'll do my homework as soon as I'm back."

"I don't care about your homework. I care about you. Be safe, OK?"

"I'm only walking the dog, Mum. Chill out."

Mum rubbed her eyes then looked at Archie. "But Huxley is Dad's dog, isn't he? Dad chose him. He walks him. Feeds him."

Archie tightened the lead, and tightened the lead, cutting off the blood supply to his fingers.

"Dad took him, sweetheart. I'm sorry. Huxley's gone too."

6

Archie left the house by the front door, holding the lead as if Huxley were attached to it, but it hung at his side. The lack of weight was alarming, making Archie feel light-headed, as if he might float off the edge of the planet and drift away without Huxley to anchor him to the ground. Huxley was huge, a bear of a dog, and Archie could have used some of that warm bulk right now. He'd wrap his arms around Huxley's thick neck and bury his face in his fur, staying there until all of this was over.

Archie didn't want to see Dad, sitting like a guest at his own table in front of a cold plate of bangers and mash as he struggled to find the right words. Archie wanted there to be no right words, no conversation that needed to be had, no agenda for Dad's visit. He'd give anything for a normal Monday teatime, everyone talking over each other,

Dad smuggling bits of sausage to Huxley as his tail thumped on the floor.

But this was not a normal Monday so instead of walking down the drive and out onto Station Road, Archie turned back on himself and headed around the side of the house.

He crept along the lawn, keeping to the hedge. It was getting dark now. Day's eyelids were closing. Archie reached the wall at the bottom of the garden and closed his own eyes, wondering if there would ever come a day when the sun would simply fail to rise, leaving everything to the moon and the stars and the owls and the foxes and the other creatures that prowled at night. Towns would be over-run with rats, homes reduced to cobwebs by spiders that never slept. The sun would wilt to nothing like the flowers in Mum's green vase.

Perhaps it would be a relief. It was hard getting up each day, hard getting up *for* each day, and maybe the sun would be glad to opt out.

Archie climbed over the wall and there was the

track, almost as if it had been waiting for him. There was no guard to tell him he was trespassing, no barbed wire fence to stop him getting close. He could walk right up to it, walk on it, if he wanted. There was nothing to stop him, so he stepped onto the track and followed it with his gaze until it veered around a corner and disappeared from view.

Archie longed to vanish with it.

He could follow the track to Huddersfield, and then to Leeds, to York, to Newcastle and all the way up to Edinburgh where Dad used to live. He'd find that big hill where Dad had taken him on his thirteenth birthday, *Arthur's* something or other, climbing to the top to eat chips in the dark.

"I used to do this with my dad, and my dad used to do it with his dad, and his dad used to do it with *his* dad – at least, that's how the story goes," Dad had explained. They'd perched on a rock, the city twinkling below their toes. "We used to come up here on my birthday. Have cold fish and chips. Just like this."

Archie could almost smell the greasy batter. He set off at a pace, lurching forward, stumbling because there was no moon, just a smattering of dull stars that looked as if they couldn't be arsed to shine. But no matter. He'd soon be away from this place. The air was different in Scotland, Dad always said so. He'd be able to breathe up there. Archie would find Dad's old house and his old football club, which might let him play if he told them he was Dad's son. He'd track down Dad's school friends and they'd tell stories about the old Dad, the person he was before Friday.

The person Dad wanted to be, but couldn't.

"I've spent a long time wishing I was different. Trust me. Almost every day of my adult life."

Archie kept moving, but more slowly, the smell of fish and chips washed away by the rain that had started to fall. Walking to Scotland wouldn't bring Dad back. Nothing would. He'd gone, or he'd never really been here in the first place. Dad's life had been a lie, which meant that Archie was a lie too. That's how Archie felt – an illusion, as if he wasn't really here. Nothing registered, not the cold, or the wet, or the horror of the spot where Tathum had jumped.

Archie looked back at it. Tia wanted to know what he'd seen. Maybe Tathum had leaned against that tree right there? Or maybe he'd checked the track, making sure that if he jumped, it would be to his death? Was that why Tathum had chosen to do it here, where the line was long and straight and the train could hit him at full speed? He'd paced around a bit, perhaps, but mostly he'd been still. At peace. Tia would be pleased to hear that.

Archie walked on, under a bridge and out the other side, past a couple of abandoned supermarket trollies, a rusty doll's pram and a white cat, crawling in the grass. The embankment was higher now, closing in, the sides too steep to offer any sort of safety if a train made a sudden appearance. Archie checked his phone. Twenty-six minutes past five. Three minutes until the Huddersfield train was due. He waited for an explosion of adrenalin, but there was only the plod of his feet between the parallel lines and the *dink dink dink* of Huxley's lead as the metal clasp tapped against the track.

Archie wondered if Huxley could hear it, or if he sensed that Archie was in danger. Dogs were intuitive like that. Perhaps his ears were pricked and he was making a fuss, woofing and whining in Malcolm's house in Kirkburton, no one there to hear his warning.

Maisy might be in trouble, passed out after downing a bottle of cider because she didn't want to think about Dad, or perhaps Amy was packing a bag this very second to run away from home. She'd done it before when Dad had banned her from the iPad, shoving her favourite books in a rucksack and leaving a note saying Dad had ruined her life. What must Amy think of Dad now? Last time, she'd only got as far as the back garden before her anger fizzled out. It would be different tonight. She'd be furious, stomping along the road like she'd stomped up the stairs on Friday evening.

Or maybe she was stomping along the track.

Amy's bedroom was at the back of the house too.

What if she'd seen Archie jump over the wall and had followed him?

"No!" Archie's voice rang out across the night. He'd come further than he'd realised. Much further. The trees were black witches, whispering in the wind. The trollies were strange beasts, skulking in the shadows. The pram creaked as a white cat in a frilly bonnet sat up to see Archie turn around and run back the way he came. "Amy? Are you there?"

Archie waited for a reply, but there was just the sound of an engine in the distance as a signal turned from red to green.

"Shit! Amy? Amy! Can you hear me?"

Archie didn't know which way she'd walked – whether she'd turned left or right when she climbed over the wall – but he had to hope that she'd followed him, that their paths would cross as he retraced his steps. He gritted his teeth, sprinting faster than he'd ever done in any football match because the train was coming – there were its lights! – and he had to save his sister.

"Amy! Where are you?"

Archie ran, eyes wide, scanning the darkness. A bird or a bat flew out of nowhere, making him jump. It shot in front of him, and Archie hit it away then slipped on the wet metal, dropping Huxley's lead as his hands slammed against the ground. He cast about, not wanting to leave the lead behind. It was all he had left of Huxley.

But the train was coming. It chugged along, no idea that it was heading for disaster. It moved serenely, eating up the track.

Two hundred metres away.

Archie abandoned the hunt for the lead. "Amy!"

He braced himself for a crash, for his sister's petrified scream ... But no. Wherever Amy was, she must have been safe – unlike him.

One hundred metres away.

The fear vanished as quickly as it had come. The numbness it left in its wake was more noticeable for the contrast, like the silence after fireworks. Perhaps the enormity of what was about to happen was simply too big to compute. Or perhaps the strange, sudden stillness of Archie's heart was acceptance.

Yes.

Archie stood, quite calm, awaiting his fate. Mum and Dad would be proud. There was no sobbing. No drama. This was for the best.

Fifty metres away.

Forty.

It would be a relief to give himself over to the darkness. He was opting out, wilting away. Screwing the rules.

"Fuckin' da man."

It was Tia who said it in a distant corner of Archie's mind. And then she was giggling at how silly she sounded, and then she was right here by his side, standing next to Archie in the rain, her chest rising and falling as she tilted back her head and breathed in the night.

That's how Tia had looked on the football pitch, like she was breathing in the world for the first time since Tathum had died, letting herself live, choosing her life once more.

And Archie chose the same, just in time, stepping backwards as the train hurtled past, slicing Huxley's lead clean in two.

7

Everyone had eaten their bangers and mash by the time Archie got home. The only sausages left were his own. Mum was there, and Dad, sitting in his normal place as if the last few days hadn't happened. Archie might have imagined the whole thing, except there was no Huxley begging for titbits at Dad's feet.

"There you are!" Mum said. "Thank God. Where've you been?"

"Walking."

"You're drenched, love."

Archie took off his jacket. "It's raining."

"What happened to your hand?" Amy asked. "Gross."

Amy pretended to vomit in the fridge then went back to choosing a yoghurt, picking up a strawberry one and then a raspberry one and then the strawberry one once more. Archie watched, amazed that she cared this much after what had just happened on the track. But she hadn't been there, had she? It seemed impossible, but she hadn't even left the house.

"What did happen to your hand?" Mum said. "It's a mess."

Archie glanced at his arm, surprised to see blood splattered on his sleeve. "It looks worse than it is," he replied – the same words he'd used when he'd come back from his old school with a cut on his face. "*We were just play-fighting*," he'd said, and Mum had believed the lie, as she did now. "I slipped. That's all."

"You've got to be more careful, love. Here," Mum said, wetting some kitchen roll and passing it to Archie. "Put that on it."

"Did you try to top yourself?" Maisy asked, because she was here too, squashing a pea into her plate with a fork. "Slit your wrists?"

"Don't be ridiculous," Mum said. "He's got more sense than that, haven't you, Archie?"

Archie couldn't bring himself to meet Mum's eye. He sat at the table as Amy made one more yoghurt swap, picking up a purple carton before closing the fridge.

"Blueberry. *Perfecto*." Amy skipped back to her seat and cuddled up to Dad. "He's a gay, Archie. Did you know?"

Archie flushed the colour of the yoghurt pot. Everyone waited.

"Yeah," he said at last. "Sort of."

"You had no idea!" Maisy said. "I had to tell you. Talk about retarded."

"I thought you needed space," Archie muttered because if he was talking to his sister, he didn't have to look at Dad, who seemed to be holding his breath, his shoulders near his ears.

Maisy shrugged. "Mum needed me more."

"Wow. Thanks," Mum said. "That's very considerate." She turned to Archie, brushing something out of his hair. "A twig! What were you doing?"

"I told you. I slipped."

"Your uniform will need washing. That blood might

not come out," Mum said. "Mind you, I've just bought some stain remover – I must have known. Bumped into Pat in Tesco, actually," she told Dad. "First time in months. Had a good chat." If Mum was trying to make Dad jealous by talking about another man, it didn't work. Dad wasn't listening. "I got your ingredients for Food Tech too, Arch." Mum smiled at him. "Pop your sausages in the microwave, there's a good lad."

Archie did as he was told, even though he wasn't hungry. There was a beep and a whirr. The sausages started to spin. Archie's head, too.

This wasn't right.

Actually, it was *too* right, too normal. Dad put the plates in the dishwasher. Maisy fiddled with her phone. Amy licked the yoghurt lid.

"Are you disappointed?" Amy asked when Archie returned to the table with his plate. "That's OK. We all are. But we're not disappointed in Dad. There's a difference." These weren't her words. They were Mum's words, and Archie clenched his teeth, irritated to hear them second hand. Amy stuck her spoon in her yoghurt. "This isn't Dad's fault, OK? Some people are born with it."

"You make it sound like an affliction," Dad muttered. "Which it has been, at times. A burden."

Mum squeezed Dad's arm as he sat back down. "One that you don't have to carry anymore."

"Some monkeys are gay," Amy went on, stirring the yoghurt. "And also Albus Dumbledore. So it's very natural, all right?"

It might have been comforting if Archie had heard Mum saying it, but it sounded odd coming from Amy. He couldn't take her seriously, like the time she dressed up in Mum's jewellery and Dad's tie, playing at being grown up but getting it wrong. It made a joke out of the whole thing, one that Mum and Dad seemed to find funny as they shared an amused look over the top of Amy's head. Maisy was smiling too. That, more than anything, took Archie by surprise.

Perhaps the train had hit Archie, after all, and he'd woken up in a different universe where everyone was too damn reasonable. He wanted to shake them, shake the whole kitchen, smash plates and hurl cups and take an axe to the table where they were all sitting so nicely like nothing was broken.

"Gravy?" Mum asked as she poured.

"No," Archie replied.

"Oops. Oh well, sorry." She didn't sound it. She didn't look it, either. None of them did. There was something warm in the air and it wasn't just steam from the onion gravy. Archie shivered, feeling colder than he had done on the track.

Mum put a white box on the table.

"Apple pie!" Dad said. "You're spoiling us."

No one flinched at his use of that word. Archie waited for it, willing Maisy to chuck down her fork and storm upstairs, or Amy to burst into tears and ask Dad why he was saying such things when he had no right.

There was no *us*. No family.

No such thing as this happy ending that was playing out in front of Archie's eyes. He sat back, refusing to join in the act.

"You didn't tell me there was ice cream," Amy

groaned as Mum took some from the freezer. "You said it was apple pie! That's why I chose this." She bashed the yoghurt pot with her spoon.

"Relax! You can have some," Mum said. "For being such a good girl today." Amy beamed, and it was easy as that. One scoop of ice cream was all it took. "Honestly, you've been amazing. All of you."

Dad nodded. "Best kids in the world."

Maisy rolled her eyes, but not very far, bringing them back to Dad. "Lots of my friends are gay. Well, two of them. So, you know. It's cool. Love is love, and all that."

"Yeah?" Dad asked.

"Yeah," Maisie replied. "As long as we can still see you."

"Of course you can. Whenever you like. We're still a family," Dad said, grabbing Maisy's hand.

Amy went cross-eyed and stuck out her tongue. "A family of freaks."

Dad laughed, grabbing Amy's hand too. "Which family isn't?"

Archie pressed the cut on his palm, digging his thumb into his broken flesh.

"But we'll stick together," Dad said. "Always. Right, Arch?" Dad seemed happy enough with Archie's silence. "Good lad. I know this is a shock. I've had thirty years to come to terms with it. You lot have had thirty seconds. I get that. I'm not expecting miracles. We can go at your speed. Take it slow. But you've been awesome today. All of you. Your mum, especially."

"Well, I've had twenty years to come to terms with it." Mum laughed and Dad did too, their eyes full of tears that Archie didn't understand. "I'm relieved to tell you the truth. Bloody relieved. That's what I told Pat. Probably made me sound crazy, but I feel as if –" She waved her hands in the air like something was fluttering away and Archie thought of the black thing by the track that had shot out of an unseen bush. "Something's lifted, you know? Something's gone."

"It's been a burden for you too, I guess. Well, we're free of it now," Dad said, as the thing with black wings flew around the kitchen before dropping like a dead weight onto Archie's chest.

||1

It was Tia's idea to partner up in Food Tech.

"You don't mind, do you, Jared?" Tia asked as Miss Banks hurried around the classroom, sorting everyone into pairs.

Miss Banks clapped her hands. "Come on, people! Look lively!"

"Me and Archie need to talk, that's all."

"We do?" Archie said. "Now?"

He wanted to, of course he did, but a pair of black eyes was watching his every move. Archie hadn't seen Leon since he'd run off with Tia to the playing field. They hadn't had the same lessons, and when Archie had gone to the canteen at lunchtime, his friends hadn't been there. But now Leon was sitting at the table they normally shared in Food Tech. It was an invitation, or a challenge. Either way, Archie felt as if he should accept.

"Yes, now. I've got some more questions. *About my brother?*" Tia whispered this last bit.

"What about Leon?" Archie muttered.

"I'm sure he can cope without you for one lesson. Right, Leon?"

Leon didn't reply. He was perched on his normal stool, staring at Archie without blinking. Archie had been preparing himself for all sorts that morning – a load of insults, a dead leg or two – but not this. This was unnerving.

"I can't just leave him," Archie said in a low voice.

Tia rolled her eyes. "He can partner up with Jared."

"Yes please," Jared replied, slinging his silver rucksack onto Leon's table. "Come on, sexy. Let's bake some brownies."

"Is that all right?" Archie asked Leon. "Just for today, yeah? Sorry."

Leon made no sign that he'd heard him. He just carried on sitting there, on the edge of his stool, waiting. Something was going to happen, Archie could

feel it, but he didn't have time to worry about that
because Tia had linked his arm.

"That one over there." She pulled Archie away
from Leon, dragging him to an empty table where they
could be alone. Sort of. Alone enough to share a shy
smile.

"Hi."

"Hi."

Tia slipped an apron over her head. "Do me up,
will you?"

She presented her back to Archie, and there was
the bra strap again, long and straight and oh-so blue.
He thought of trickling streams and gushing rivers
and wading into a warm sea that lapped at his legs,
his thighs, his groin.

He was all groin, unable to remember how to tie a
bow.

"Just a sec," Archie said, wondering how men ever
got to the point where they could casually undress
a girl when it was this overwhelming to clothe one.
"Sorry."

Tia shook him off. "I'll do it. It's not that hard."

Archie hid his embarrassment by opening his rucksack and getting out his ingredients. On the next table, Leon did the same. It was as if he'd been waiting for Archie to make the first move, but that made no sense – at least, it didn't until Archie looked around. In front of Leon was a Tesco bag, exactly the same as Archie's.

"Snap," Leon mouthed, and that's when Archie remembered that Leon's mum was called Patricia.

Pat, to her old friends.

8

Tia's questions about her brother were endless. She wanted to know everything – the dates Archie had spotted Tathum by the track, how long he'd stayed there, what he'd done and what his mood had seemed to be.

"I don't know, OK?" Archie said at last as he took a tray of chocolate brownies out of the oven. They were burned to a crisp. He wafted away the smoke, trying to think – but not about Tathum. It was vital to recall what Mum had said about Pat. Had she mentioned what they'd discussed? "I don't know what he was feeling," Archie told Tia.

Archie put the brownies on the table.

"I just mean was he crying or anything?" Tia went on, not looking at the brownies. "Did he seem angry? Was he ranting or chucking stuff?"

"He was just standing there," Archie replied.

Tia frowned. "You said before that he was pacing."

"He paced for a bit and then he stood there, OK?"

"Which time?" Tia asked.

"What?"

"You said you saw him twice."

Archie bunged all the bowls in the sink and started to wash up. "It's hard to remember. It was, like, a year ago –"

"A year ago tomorrow. I know." Tia grabbed a glass jug and chucked it in the sink, splashing Archie's shirt.

They didn't speak for a few seconds.

Archie shook his head. "Sorry."

"Twenty-nine minutes past nine on the first of November, to be precise."

Archie didn't have to look at Tia to know she was on the edge of tears. He could hear it in her voice as she stomped around, tidying up noisily. "Excuse me for wanting to know what Tathum was thinking. For trying to work out what the hell was going through his mind."

"I'm sorry." Archie turned around, his hands dripping wet. A puddle formed on the floor. "I didn't mean it like that."

"Working your magic there, Archibald?" Leon called as he took his own chocolate brownies out of the oven. They were perfect. "Good with the ladies, I see. Like father, like son, eh?" Leon smirked. "Chip off the old block."

Tia glanced at Archie, who wished he could melt into the puddle on the floor. "What's he talking about?"

"He hasn't told you?" Leon gasped and tutted in mock surprise. "Oh, me and my big mouth."

"Told me what? Archie?"

The room swam in front of Archie's eyes. He reached out to steady himself, his hand slamming on the sink as his legs gave way. They felt heavy, or light, full of blood, or completely empty. He was here, and not here, floating above a scene he hadn't even witnessed in the supermarket. Mum was telling Pat everything, and Archie wanted to yell at her to stop, but he was powerless.

And now Leon knew. There was no denying it. The truth was out.

"Are you all right?" Tia asked. "What's up?"

Archie turned back to the washing up, the cut on his palm stinging. It must have re-opened when he'd grabbed the sink. It hurt. It hurt so much and he wanted it to stop.

"One minute left to get this room sorted," Miss Banks called. "Come on! It's twenty-nine minutes past ten."

Archie stared at the clock. Somewhere near his house, the Huddersfield train would be speeding along the track. Archie could almost feel it, vibrating under his feet.

\|\|

As usual, the bell rang long before Miss Banks dismissed the class. The room had to be spotless before anyone could leave. Miss Banks inspected each table, checking the equipment was clean and in the correct drawers. Tia was restless, jiggling her legs, but Archie was still. As Miss Banks moved around the room, Archie willed her to find more crumbs, more smears of chocolate, more unwashed baking trays.

Jack and Mo were waiting in the corridor.

If Leon knew, they probably did too.

Miss Banks checked the sinks then nodded. "OK. Off you go."

"So I thought we could go to the track today after school," Tia said. "It'll be a lot easier for you to explain if I can see it for myself. What lesson have you got last? Archie, are you listening?"

He was trying to, but he couldn't make sense of her words.

Tia shook his sleeve. "Miss Banks said we can go."

Archie wasn't sure he could stand up. He was so tired, he didn't know if he could survive the next few seconds, let alone the rest of the day. Jared joined them at their table as Leon moved with the crowd towards the door.

"That boy's a dick," Jared murmured. "But he's got a very fine arse."

Tia shook Archie's sleeve again. "Come on! We've only got five minutes of break left."

Archie closed his eyes, longing to curl up in a ball and go to sleep, but he had to move. It was time to go.

"So what do you reckon?" Tia said. "Tonight?"

"All right." Archie could barely lift his feet, or his bag, which seemed to have doubled in weight. It was grey, just like Leon's. He'd chosen it for that reason.

"It's a date," Tia said. "Not a date. But yeah. We'll do it tonight."

"Do what?" Jack said as they stepped into the corridor. A light buzzed, flickering on and off as if the world was running out of electricity. Archie wished it would. A plunge into sudden darkness would be a relief. "Not bone? That wouldn't work. Archie wouldn't be able to get it up."

"Don't be so immature," Tia said. She linked Archie's arm and tried to drag him away, but he had no energy to move. He was a dead weight, dragging her down, dragging everyone down, his family most of all. His sisters had accepted Dad. Mum, too. It was just Archie getting in the way. "Let's go outside."

"It's true," Mo said. "Jack's right. Archie's only pretending to like you to get closer to Jared."

"Shut up," Tia said.

"What's all this?" Leon asked. He was leaning against the wall, his hands in his pockets. "Archie likes Jared?"

"Oh yeah," Mo replied, as Archie felt himself go red. "You weren't there yesterday. Archie told us he was gay."

"No, I didn't," Archie said quickly, as Leon raised an eyebrow. "That's not what I said."

"It is! That's why you wouldn't get off with Izzie at the party," Mo went on. "You said it yourself." He put on a girly voice. "*I can't. I like someone else.* We didn't know who it was at the time, but now –" Mo drew back an imaginary arrow and shot it at Jared's head. "*Bingo.*"

Jared sighed. "Don't you mean *bullseye?*"

"Bingo. Bullseye. Whatever," Leon said. "It makes perfect sense."

"No, it doesn't." That was Jared again. His eyes were on Leon's, blue taking on black. "I'm gay."

Jack clutched his chest. "No! Really?"

"So I should know. Archie doesn't give me the vibes, but you do." Jared was staring at Leon. "You give me all the right feels." There was a deadly silence, apart from the buzz of the light. "In all the right places." Jared smiled. "But maybe that's just wishful thinking."

Jack burst out laughing. "You just got owned, mate!"

"Shut the fuck up," Leon snarled, and the laughter died instantly. He stepped up to Jared, who didn't flinch. "Say it again."

"You give me all the right feels," Jared repeated. "I saw how you were looking at me in that classroom."

Leon grabbed Jared by the scruff of the neck and shoved him against the wall. "Say it again." His arm was crushing Jared's throat.

"Leon! No!" Tia said. "Archie, do something!"

"Say it again!"

"You," Jared began, fighting for breath, "you ..."

"Yeah, go on," Leon said, pressing down harder on Jared's throat. "Let's hear it."

"You ... give ... me ..." Jared spluttered. He kneed Leon hard in the crotch, squirming free as Tia whooped. *"All the right feels!"* Jared cried in Leon's face. *"In all the right places."*

"Amazing!" Tia said. "Take that, dickhead."

Leon was doubled up on the floor. Jack and Mo hovered above him, unsure what to do.

"Fuck off, all of you," Leon said. "Pricks."

Archie didn't need telling twice. He hurried away with Tia and Jared, bursting out of the corridor into a blazing autumn day as if their victory had set the whole world alight. Archie wouldn't have been surprised to see a rainbow shining in the sky. Jared was talking at top speed, high on the moment, Tia re-enacting the knee in the balls as Archie walked a couple of steps behind. This was their victory, not his. He'd done nothing, and his grey bag felt heavier than ever as Jared's rucksack sparkled in the sunshine.

9

Archie kept his head down for the rest of the morning. It wasn't hard. He'd had a lot of practice. His world shrank to the space just in front of his feet.

At lunchtime, Tia had netball and Jared was busy, so Archie found himself alone in the library with his Geography homework. As he calculated six-figure grid references on a map, he felt the scar on his face, wondering if the last few months had even happened. Archie might have moved schools, but he'd ended up in the same place. All routes seemed to lead back here. Archie bent over the map, studying the towns and villages, putting his finger on Shepley and then moving it to Kirkburton, pushing down to crush Malcolm's house. He jumped his finger to Huddersfield and then to Halifax and then to Settle at the top of the map. Heading up there would make no difference. Everything was linked by roads and pathways. There was only one way to cut the ties.

Tathum had done it and now no one could get to him. No one could find him. Wherever Tathum was, he was free. Archie lifted his finger above the map. Dad looked up from Kirkburton. Mum called his name from Shepley. Leon searched every street, every building, but Archie had gone.

|||

Archie had been waiting for it all day, but the final bell still made him jump. He'd survived. Leon hadn't said a word about Dad, not even when Archie had seen him in the playground, out of sight of any teachers. Mo and Jack hadn't said anything, either. Maybe Leon hadn't told them. Perhaps Archie wasn't the only one trying to keep his head down.

No question, Archie owed Jared, big time.

And now – Tia.

Archie jogged to the main gate to meet her. The air was cold, slicing through his lungs. Archie had been sinking all day, going under, but now he breathed. It was miraculous, the way oxygen found a way in, how his heart kept beating, thudding even, as he lifted his eyes for the first time in hours. Tia was sitting on a wall, her pink laces glowing in the pale sun.

"Hey," Archie said. "You ready?" He was fizzy, full of bubbles that popped in his stomach as she nodded. He pointed down the road. "That way."

Tia set off without speaking. She wasn't crying, but a crumpled tissue in her hand told Archie she had been all afternoon. He shook his head. He'd do anything for her – step out in front of that lorry, right there, if it would save her life. Jump under that bus. Take her down to the track and say whatever she needed to hear to be happy. Never mind Tathum. It was Tia's peace that was important now.

"Down here."

They hurried along Station Road, past the turning for Archie's house, heading for an old stone bridge where the road dwindled to a lane and then a footpath that vanished over fields. Archie stopped, waiting to show Tia the track from the top of the bridge, but she glanced backwards then slipped under a barbed wire fence.

"Where are you going?" Archie said, as Tia slid down the embankment on her bum before dropping onto the track. Archie peered over the bridge. "Tia?"

"What? There isn't a train for ages. Come on!" she called. "I thought you wanted to show me."

"From up here. Not down there. *Shit. Shit!*" Archie was following her. Of course he was, stumbling down to land in a heap on the track. Tia was sitting on her heels under the bridge. Archie's footsteps echoed as he entered. "This is a bad idea. People walk their dogs around here all the time. My dad does!" he said, before remembering that wasn't true anymore.

"Your dad won't see us down here."

Archie kicked a stone. "Fuck him." He crouched down, leaning back on the damp wall. Of all the places he'd imagined ending up alone with Tia – and he'd imagined a lot – he'd never pictured this. It wasn't just the trolleys and the rusty doll's pram. It was the graffiti. The litter. The poo bags. Still. It was better than nothing, private and quiet – so quiet, Archie could hear Tia breathing. It sped up, became a laugh.

"Jared!"

Archie grinned. "I know."

"Unbelievable, wasn't it?"

"Yeah. He's not as weedy as he looks."

"Jared, weedy?" Tia said. "Are you kidding? He's been doing martial arts for years." Tia karate-chopped a rusty cider can by her feet. "Tathum would have been proud."

"Did he do martial arts too?"

For some reason, Tia smirked. "Something like that."

"I thought he played football."

"What, did you read that in the paper?" Tia didn't sound so impressed now.

"Well, yeah. I didn't know him," Archie said as he picked at some moss.

"No one did." Tia hit the can. "People only remember the headlines. *Talented footballer.*

Straight-A student. Loving son. It doesn't mean anything. It's not real." She held up the can. "He liked to drink, actually. And he was horrible to Mum sometimes. The papers should have said, '*He was a grumpy bastard, who Mum had to drag out of bed because he hated school.*' At least it would have been the truth." She sighed. "Instead there were photos of all those white flowers. Like he was royalty. Not a normal person. Not my brother."

Archie wanted to ask about the red rose, but he wasn't meant to have seen her lay it by the track so he kept quiet.

"I'm starting to forget too," Tia said. "That sounds awful, doesn't it?"

"No," Archie replied. "Not really."

"It's just, you kind of do. Like, how his face moved when he talked. I've got videos on my phone, so I know how he looked when he was messing about for five seconds, or whatever. But not how he looked when he was pissed off, or laughing at the TV, or just hanging out in my room."

"So you were close then?" Archie asked.

Tia smiled. "Don't get me wrong. We fought. Properly wrestled, sometimes. But we also played a lot of *Grand Theft Auto* on Friday nights."

Archie laughed. "No way."

"Hell, yeah! I'm shit-hot at stealing cars. We'd stay up all night. He'd drink a bit. Cheap cider, like this." Tia tossed the can away and it bounced off the wall, clattering on the track. "Even when he had a game the next day. So that was your dedicated footballer." She stared at the can. "It wasn't his, was it? The cider?"

"What?"

"When you saw him? Was he drinking? That can's the brand he liked."

Archie looked at Tia's eager face. It didn't feel so easy to lie now. "We should move." He stood up. "We don't want to risk anything. A train could –"

"There isn't one for half an hour."

"What if it's early?" Archie said. "We should –"

"Why did you bring me here?" The anger in

Tia's voice shocked Archie. She shot to her feet and started unbuttoning her shirt. A dark triangle of skin appeared at the base of her neck. Archie could see her collarbone. A beauty spot on her chest. "Is it for this?" Tia asked. "Is that what you want? I'll show you, if that's the deal?"

"What? No!" Archie held up a hand to shield his eyes. He didn't want to see her, not like this.

"I don't mind. If this is what it takes, fine. Look! Touch them, if you want!" Tia yanked her shirt open, and there was the dark blue bra, silky and smooth, a delicate frill arching over each breast.

"Put them away, Tia." Archie turned his back. "Seriously. Do up your shirt."

"It's true then, is it? What Jack and Mo said? You prefer Jared to me? You must do if you won't even look."

Archie stared at the wall, his face on fire.

"What the fuck is wrong with you, Archie?"

The question bounced around the tunnel, around the bones of Archie's skull. He'd be hearing its echo for days.

"I just don't want to," he said. It was true. His lack of desire was unnerving. He waited for the familiar stirrings, but there was nothing, no Tia Effect at all.

"Fine!" Tia spat. "I'll put them away if you find them so disgusting."

When Archie turned back round, Tia's shirt was buttoned up all wrong, her tie to one side. She looked down at herself. "Oh God," she sobbed. "Sorry. What an idiot. Me, not you. You're –" she gestured at Archie "– lovely."

"I'm not," Archie mumbled because if he were lovely, he would never have lied to Tia in the first place. It was his fault they were here. This – all of it – was his doing. "Let's go. Please?"

Tia sniffed. "I just need to know that he was happy." Tears streamed down her face, dripped off her chin. "That's all I want to know."

"He was all right, OK?" Archie said because he couldn't stand it a second longer. "He wasn't upset. He wasn't angry. He was calm."

"But you said he was pacing." Tia wiped her nose

on the back of her hand. "That sounds pissed off to me. Like he was angry."

"I meant walking, really."

"Where?"

Archie pointed down the track. "Along there," he said, trying to be vague to make it less of a lie. "He was checking it out, maybe. But there was no big drama. No tears."

Tia sniffed again. "You promise?"

Archie had to look away. "I promise. Now can we go?"

Tia nodded and they trudged out of the tunnel into gloom. The sun had given up on the day. Archie wouldn't blame it if it never rose again.

10

Archie took off his jacket in the hall as his sisters appeared in their coats.

"Where are you two going?" Archie asked.

"Where have you been?" Mum called. "You're back late."

"I had to see a teacher about something." He watched Amy pull on a pair of shiny black boots, her tongue sticking out as she hopped about, yanking at a zip.

Mum popped her head around the door. "You're not in trouble, are you?"

"No. They don't fit," Archie told Amy.

She flopped onto her back, her leg flailing about as she tugged at the boot.

"But they're my best! That's what you always say, Mum. They're your best. *Save them for something special.*"

"Where are you going?" Archie asked again.

Maisy was a cloud of perfume wafting past Archie as she grabbed her bag off the banister. "Dad's."

"You're invited too," Mum said. "He called about half an hour ago. Said you could all go round for tea."

"Not hungry," Archie replied.

"Dad would like to see you anyway."

"Homework." Archie started on the stairs. Mum followed, almost clipping his heels as she chased after him.

"You can do it there. Dad said there's a desk. A spare room so you can stay over at the weekend."

"All of us together?" Archie turned to face Mum on the landing. He wasn't sure when it had happened, but he was taller than she was. "In one room?"

Mum frowned. "Don't start, OK. Not now. Amy's excited."

Archie glanced down the stairs to see his sister hobbling around the hall, trying to get used to the boots. "They're fine! Comfy." Amy beamed up at Archie, who forced a smile.

"They look good!"

"Come, Arch. Please?" Amy said. "Dad wants to show us our room. There are three beds. Mine's got a teddy on it! Malcolm bought it for me. And he got you some blue covers from Next."

"That's a bit weird," Archie muttered to Mum. "Who is he, this guy? Why is he buying me covers?"

"I know him," Mum said. "Do you think I'd let you go to a stranger's house? He's nice."

Archie breathed out. There it was again – the urge to shake something until it broke. This time it was Mum. Archie wanted to crack her, to make her scream and shout and sob that Dad had gone. His whole body craved it, his ribs trembling as the thing with black wings broke free. It burst from him, swooping, searching for somewhere to rest.

But Mum wasn't available and the creature let out a desolate cry as it returned to Archie's chest.

"Really nice," Mum went on. "I like him. He works in the library. Has done for years."

"It's not that dude with the knitted jumpers, is it?" Archie asked.

"That's him."

"No way. He's about seventy!"

"He's fifty-one." Mum smiled. "Give him a chance.
For Dad's sake, eh?"

Outside, there was a beep. "He's here!" Amy
squealed, clapping her hands together. "I'm going to
show him my sticker!"

She sped out of the door as fast as she could in boots
that didn't fit. Archie could hear her giggling as Dad
spun her in a circle. "Faster! Faster! Again! Again!"

"She got a sticker for telling her class that Dad's
gay," Mum said, following Archie into his room. "He
was her show-and-tell."

"Good for her." Archie put his phone on to charge
then dropped onto his bed, pulling the pillow over his
face. It was blissfully cold, beautifully dark.

"She took in a photo of him. One of a monkey too.
And a picture of Dumbledore off the internet, only it
was Gandalf. I didn't tell her." Mum sounded amused.
"You can't fault her guts. And you know what, Archie?
Everyone was fine with it."

Archie pulled down the pillow. "They're seven, Mum. They still believe in Santa."

"Maisy told her friends too."

"They're girls."

"Not all of them are."

"What did you tell Pat?" Archie asked.

"The truth, Arch. Just the truth."

"She's Leon's mum. Leon knows."

"Good. You can talk to him about it. It's nothing to be ashamed of."

"I'm not ashamed," Archie said, but it was a lie so huge he almost choked on it. He wished he could show off a picture of Dad at school, hold it up for his friends to see, stick it on his bag next to an extra-bright rainbow. That's what Jared would do, but Archie didn't have his courage. Or Maisy's. Or even his little sister's.

Only Archie had the problem. It was his, and his alone.

"Are you sure?" Mum said. "I hope not. We're proud of Dad, OK? Always. It wasn't easy to do what he did. He's still my best friend. He's still your father. There's no great tragedy here."

"*So why do I feel like shit?*" Archie wanted to ask, but how could he say those words when Mum was so insistent that everything was fine? He yanked the pillow back over his face.

"You're not sulking, are you?" Mum said. "I can't be doing with that today, love."

Archie continued to hide.

"Don't be silly, Arch. You've got to be strong for your sisters. They look up to you. They do! I know it might not feel like it, but –"

A knock at the door stopped Mum in her tracks. She poked Archie in the ribs. "Let's go and say hi to Dad. Come on." There was another knock, and then silence. "You'll feel better for seeing him." Mum grabbed Archie's hand and pulled him to his feet, groaning with the effort. Archie felt it again, how heavy he was, how much he weighed Mum down.

A third knock echoed around the house.

"Why doesn't he just come in," Mum muttered.

"He doesn't have to stand in the porch, like a stranger. Go on. After you, love."

Archie trudged down the stairs and opened the front door, forcing himself to say, "Hello."

The word died in his throat. It wasn't Dad.

111

"Hello, Archie." Leon cocked his head to one side – the head he was meant to be keeping down for fear of what Jared might do – and gave Archie a dazzling smile. "Surprise."

"A lovely surprise!" Mum said. "We were just talking about you."

"Were you?" Leon asked. His eyes didn't leave Archie's face. "No wonder my ears were burning." He touched his earlobe and winced. "Hot."

Mum snorted. "Give over. It was all good. I was just telling Archie how you need your friends at times like this. People you can trust."

Leon looked at Mum for the first time. "That's why

I'm here, Mrs Maxwell." He stepped into the house. "For Archie." Leon reached out and squeezed Archie's shoulder, his fingers digging into his bones. "He wasn't himself at school today. I thought he could use a visitor."

"That's kind," Mum said.

Archie's scar tingled as a memory came back to him. He was standing in this hall, blood trickling down his cheek, willing Mum to see past his lies when he told her everything was fine at school. But she took him at his word. She took everyone at their word, which was why she was offering Leon a drink.

"Coke? Lemonade? Blackcurrant?" Mum walked into the kitchen. "Cup of tea?"

"Tea would be perfect," Leon replied, taking off his jacket and dropping it on the floor. "Get that, will you, Archie?" he added in a low voice. "I am your guest."

Archie kicked the jacket to one side. "What are you doing here?"

"Sugar? Milk? Little bit? Lots of?" Mum called.

Leon pounded his forehead with his fist. "*Blah.*

Blah. Blah. God, your mum bangs on a bit. *Milk please, Mrs Maxwell,*" he said in a completely different voice. *"Just a splash."*

"That's how I like it too! You boys go on upstairs. I'll bring it up." Mum returned to the hall, rattling a tin of biscuits. "Here, take one of these."

"Ooh, chocolate. My favourite," Leon said.

"Mine too," Mum replied. She grinned at Leon as she popped one in her mouth.

It was Leon who walked up the stairs first, taking his time, running a finger up the banister.

"I think I can remember which one's your room. Here," Leon said, pushing the door with his foot. "The one that stinks of cock. Probably not yours. Jared's? Or your dad's? Is he a paedo as well as gay?"

Anger rushed through Archie's veins. He shoved Leon against a bookshelf. "Leave my dad out of this," Archie said, but his grip wasn't tight enough and Leon broke free. He started to slow-clap, his hands in Archie's face.

"Wow, I'm impressed. Was that a bit of spunk?

Pun intended." Leon smirked. "Fighting spirit, Archie!
I like it. Give me a *grrrr*. Like a big, brave tiger. Go
on!"

Archie slumped down on the chair by his desk
as Leon moved around the room, looking under
magazines, nudging Archie's clothes to the side with
his foot. "Where is it?" Leon asked.

"Where's what?" Archie said.

"Your phone."

"Why?"

"I'm asking the questions here, Archibald. Tell me
where it is."

Archie's eyes betrayed him.

"Aha!" Leon unplugged the phone from the
charger. "Now, what did you want to say to Jared?"
He drummed his fingers against his chin, pretending
to think.

"Put it down, Leon."

"Or what? You gonna fight me, pussy cat?"

"Tea!" Mum said, backing into the room. Two cups
steamed next to a plate of biscuits on a pink tray.

"Just in case you want another one." Mum put down the tray on the only bit of space on Archie's desk. "Gosh, Leon. You'll have to excuse the mess. Archie's a mucky pup."

Leon's tongue touched his top lip as he hid a smile. "He is, isn't he? Who does Archie get that from then? You or –"

"His dad," Mum said.

Leon's face was jubilant. "Really? Two mucky pups together."

Mum nodded. "Yes, they are." She looked from Archie to Leon and beamed. "It's nice to see you, love. Isn't it, Archie? Didn't I say? People don't mind. Not your true friends, anyway." She ruffled Archie's hair. For a horrifying moment, Archie thought she might do the same to Leon. Instead, she patted him on the shoulder. "Right. I'll leave you two to it. Don't let your tea get cold!" Mum wiggled her fingers and then she was gone.

"Fucking hell," Leon said. "Is she always that chirpy? And what are these?" He picked up a biscuit, sniffed it then chucked it back down on the plate. "Lidl's finest, eh?"

"Give me my phone," Archie said.

"Sure." Leon tossed it across the room. Archie was so surprised, he made no attempt to catch it. "Don't get your hopes up, dickhead," Leon muttered. "I need you to type in the passcode."

"I'm not doing that."

"Yes, you are," Leon said, lying down on Archie's bed. He crossed his ankles and put his hands behind his head. "You're going to do it now and then you're going to message Jared to meet you at the school field tomorrow. Bright and early. Before lessons."

Archie didn't pick up his phone. "And why would I do that?"

"To teach that little prick a lesson," Leon replied, his face hard. "That faggot embarrassed me today and I can't have that. But I don't want to get in trouble, do I? I'm not a meat-head, which is why it's so good that you owe me a favour."

"I don't owe you shit, Leon."

110

"Oh, but you do, Archibald. I kept quiet today. I could have made your life hell, but I didn't." Leon swung one leg off the bed, and then the other, standing up slowly. "Start typing."

"I'm not –"

Leon moved towards him, putting one hand on each arm of the chair so that his body formed a bridge over Archie's. "If you don't, I'll tell the whole world that your dad fucks other men. That he loves it up the arse." Leon leaned closer to Archie, muttering in his ear. "That he likes nothing more than a big dick rammed down his throat. Got it?" Leon pulled away, breathing over Archie's face. "Now pick up the phone and tell that freak to meet you at the school field."

"And then what?" Archie replied in a voice that didn't seem his own. He had never sounded more afraid, more cowed, and his stomach curled in on itself, clenching in shame. "What do you want me to do?"

Leon smiled, his lips so close to Archie's, they almost touched. "I want you to beat that little poof to a pulp."

11

Archie did as Leon asked. A couple of minutes later, Jared replied, agreeing to meet, but Archie didn't intend to ever return to school. It wasn't a decision, exactly. It was a fact. He wouldn't go back. He couldn't. Hurting Jared wasn't an option, but neither was giving Leon a reason to tell the whole school about Dad.

Archie walked to the window, pulled by something beyond the glass. There was no way out apart from *the* way out. It didn't come as a shock. He'd half-known that this would be his fate.

"I look forward to seeing Jared's mashed-up face in the morning then," Leon said. "You better not chicken out, Archibald. That stupid little faggot's got it coming to him."

Archie turned away from the window. It wasn't easy. He was drawn to the darkness, part of it now. He belonged out there, with the track.

"You do know this means he won, right?" he told Leon. "Whatever happens tomorrow, Jared got under your skin, not the other way around."

"He got under nowhere!" The outburst was brutal. Spit flew from Leon's mouth and landed on his chin. He wiped it away with a snarl. "He's the one who's scared of me!"

Archie looked at Leon for a few seconds. "So why are you here?"

Leon didn't have an answer for that.

Exhaustion washed over Archie, wave after relentless wave. He went under, no longer fighting it, no longer even trying. He let go – of the past, of the future, of everything. All that remained was this moment, right here, and he was unwilling to share it with Leon.

"Piss off, will you?" Archie said. "Close the door on your way out."

Archie started to tidy up, picking up his clothes off the floor. Hoody. Jeans. Jogging bottoms. He didn't want to leave Mum with a mess tomorrow. He grabbed a red T-shirt. He'd never wear it again. The thought didn't strike him as sad – it was just another fact. He wouldn't wear the T-shirt, or those socks, or that jumper. He folded the clothes, packing his life away in the drawer.

Next, Archie took the cups to the bathroom, tipping cold tea down the sink. He ate the biscuits then carried the tray downstairs. Mum would be pleased to see everything had gone. He could at least give her that, even if he'd failed her when it came to Dad.

|||

It seemed odd to have breakfast the next morning, but Archie didn't know what else to do. He'd never killed himself before. He poured Coco Pops into a bowl then ate them quietly. His sisters were busy upstairs. Mum was in the shower. Archie savoured the noise – Mum's terrible singing, the splash of water, the whirr of the fan. He hadn't heard any of it for years. It was strange what you grew used to, and strange what you treasured when you only had seventy-seven minutes left to live.

Archie washed out his bowl. If it had been a normal morning, he would have left it on the side, but he didn't want Mum getting sentimental over a few mushy Coco Pops when she found out what he'd done. His clothes were tidy. His desk was neat, the drawers almost empty, except for a pen and a sheet of paper that he would need before the end. Anything personal was stuffed in a bin liner under his bed. He'd get rid of it before he got rid of himself, saving Mum a job.

Archie returned to his room, one last time. It didn't smell like his. He'd spent hours on it the night before, hardly sleeping, finding comfort in the monotony of cleaning his windows, putting his books in alphabetical order, polishing his football trophies and packing them away in a box that he'd put in the loft. It would be easy now to makeover his room, take out his single bed and replace it with a double. Dad and Malcolm could come to stay whenever they liked.

His sisters would love that. They'd sit together around the kitchen table, eating bangers and mash.

They'd forget about Archie, soon enough. That's what Tia had said. *"I'm starting to forget too ... It's just, you kind of do."*

Archie wished these were the only words he could recall. But Tia was unbuttoning her shirt, pulling it open, and he was refusing to look.

"What the fuck is wrong with you, Archie?"

"Everything," he whispered as he sat at his desk to write the note.

There wasn't a lot to say. Mum would know why he'd done it. She'd have felt it too as she'd pulled him to his feet – how heavy he was, how much of a burden. She'd miss Archie, but she'd be liberated, set free. So would Dad. He wouldn't have to take it slow. He'd be able to stroll hand-in-hand with Malcolm down Kirkburton high street, if that's what he wanted. And Dad deserved that. He deserved to be happy, even if Archie wasn't brave enough to witness it.

Archie scribbled *Sorry*. And then *I love you*. And

finally *All of you* so Dad would know it wasn't his fault. He folded the note, put it under his pillow – and that was it. There was nothing left to do. It was time to leave.

He was just about to get the bin liner from under his bed when Mum walked in.

"Archie!" She grinned as she stood there in her dressing gown, her hair wrapped in a towel. "Look at it in here! I can't believe it." She ran a finger over the window sill. "Dust free! And you've even made your bed!" She patted his cheek. "Well done, Arch. It helped, did it? Seeing Leon?"

"It made a few things clear." Archie's voice was flat. The time for feeling sad or angry had passed. There was no past to regret. No future to dread. There was just the here and now, which was dwindling to nothing as the end drew near.

"Did it, indeed?" Mum smiled at him so tenderly, he had to look away. "Well, good. As long as you're OK now."

"I am OK," Archie replied because it seemed

important for Mum to know. "You don't have to worry."

"I'm your mother. That's my job."

"But you need to know that I'm OK," Archie said, and it was Tia he was thinking about, Tia with her endless questions about Tathum. He wanted to spare Mum that torment. "Hear it, Mum."

"I am hearing it, you daft thing. You're OK. I'm glad. Now let me go and sort out my hair before it dries funny. Do you want a lift to school? I'm dropping off your sisters."

"Nah. It's cool. I'll walk."

"All right, sweetheart." Mum pecked him on the cheek. "See you tonight."

A lump formed in Archie's throat, but he swallowed it down. "Bye, Mum."

\|\|

Archie sneaked out of the house with the bin liner and dumped it in a skip across the road. He checked his phone, taking it off *silent*. Four missed calls and a message from Jared.

Where are you? Going for a smoke in the woods.

That was good news. Archie had been worried that Leon might turn up to witness Jared's beating, but he was obviously too much of a coward, even for that. Archie sent a quick reply.

Sorry. Got held up. Don't wait for me.

Archie stared at his phone. Was that his last ever message? It didn't seem enough. He wanted to say something significant, tell Jared how he was the bravest person he'd ever known, but Archie was scared of rousing suspicion. He'd already risked too much with Mum. He needed to keep his head, but it was trickier than he'd expected. Everything was too loud, too close – even a bike trundling down the other side of the road made him jump.

Archie dropped his phone in his pocket and stood for a moment under a dull sky. There was no sun – just grey, endless grey, a huge expanse of nothing above his head. If there was a heaven, Archie hoped it would look like this. He'd float, free of gravity, free of thought.

But he had to get there first, and that wasn't so easy, after all. Archie's pulse increased, skipping a few beats, and then a few more, struggling to find a steady rhythm. It was almost time to go down to the track, but Archie wanted one final walk up Station Road, past the lamp-post where Huxley always peed and the bus stop where he'd first kissed a girl. He needed to visit his primary school too, and how about the pitch where he'd scored his first ever hat-trick? He couldn't die without reliving that memory – Dad screaming himself hoarse as Archie had chipped the keeper in the rain, headed the ball into the back of the net in the hail and volleyed it into the top left corner as it had started to snow.

Archie would never see snow again.

Never smell it. Or crunch it with his boots. Or wake up to see his curtains glow like they had done last December. Archie knew it had snowed the second he opened his eyes. The light was different in his room and there were no trains. No noise. A seven-inch silence had fallen overnight. School had been cancelled and no one could get to work, so his family had taken the sledge onto the farmer's field. Maisy had started complaining about the cold after ten minutes. Amy had lasted twenty. But Archie and Dad had sledged for hours.

That had been a really good day.

Archie jogged to a pedestrian crossing and bashed the button. He needed to climb that hill one more time. He wanted to stand at the summit and remember Dad, whooping with joy as the sledge jumped over the ramp they'd made with their bare hands, taking off their soggy gloves to shape it with their fingers.

"Nice work," Dad had said, putting his arm around Archie. "Good job, son."

Archie hit the button again, and again, but no green man appeared.

"Come on. Come on!" Archie's ears were humming, or something was – a loud, high-pitched buzz. He shook his head, but the hum stopped. He

took his phone from his pocket and looked at the
screen, but it was miles away, his hand no longer
attached to his body. Archie blinked, squinted, and
saw it was almost nine.

The green man bleeped, but it was too late. Archie
had run out of time.

Unless ...

But no.

The thought died, half-formed, a bird with no
wings. Archie had to go to the track. School wasn't an
option. By now, Leon would know Archie hadn't laid a
finger on Jared, and he'd be blabbing Archie's secret to
anyone who'd listen.

*"I'll tell the whole world that your dad fucks other
men. That he loves it up the arse. That he likes
nothing more than a big –"*

"Enough!" Archie screamed. "Enough! I've had
enough!" It was the truest thing he'd ever said. He
couldn't stand it – not for a minute, not for a second
longer – and he knew that Tia's brother had felt the
same a year ago to the day.

The track was calling Archie, calling to the black creature in his chest, promising freedom. Escape.

Archie ran.

He raced past a blur of houses, cars he hardly saw, people he ignored. And all the time, the track was calling, calling, calling, urging him onwards.

"I'm coming," Archie muttered. "I'm on my way. I'm on my way!" His words were the rhythm of the wheels. His blood was the fuel. His breath was the whistle of the train as it neared. "I'm on my way. I'm on my way. I'm on my way."

The hum was deafening now. Archie sprinted past his turning. He didn't look at his house. His home. He'd already left. He didn't belong there anymore.

He was a boy of the track – just like Tathum.

Archie skidded to a stop at the old stone bridge and ducked under the barbed wire fence. He threw himself down the embankment, landing in the middle of the track. It was waiting for him, solid and reassuring, the cold metal humming with the promise of release.

The track had summoned him, and Archie had responded.

The problem was, someone else had heard its call.

12

"Tia?"

She was sitting under the bridge, stroking the petals of a red rose.

"Hey!" Her smile was so beautiful, Archie's breath caught in his throat and fluttered there, like a trapped moth. He'd made her eyes do that, light up and sparkle. It was as if the sun had broken through the grey clouds. "I knew you'd come," Tia said.

"You did?"

"It's today, isn't it? Tathum's anniversary. That's why you're here?" Tia asked.

Archie could only nod.

"I said to myself when I was brushing my teeth, *Archie will be at the track. He gets it. He knows that I need him.*" She stood up, still smiling, but the warmth was no longer so comfortable. Archie shifted from one foot to the other. Tia held out her hands as if it was a miracle. "And here you are."

Archie shrugged. "Don't worry about it. Seriously, it's –"

"No, listen. I was an idiot yesterday. I should never have said those things. *Done* those things." She winced. "That wasn't me. Well, it was, but it wasn't, if you know what I mean?" Tia walked towards Archie, the rose at her side, the petals moving in the breeze.

"It's OK," Archie said, checking his phone. "Forget it."

09.15

He needed to find a way to make Tia leave, but she was linking his arm and pulling him along the embankment to where Tathum had jumped.

"Pretty crap tribute." Tia pointed at the cluster of white flowers. "People have lost interest, forgotten him already. Next year there'll be even less. And, finally, nothing. Apart from this." She held up the red rose. "And those, from my parents." She nudged a fancy white bouquet with her toe. "Typical. Not that I blame them. They didn't know."

126

"Know what?" Archie asked as he looked at his phone to see that another minute had passed.

"Stuff." Tia sat down, pulling Archie with her. She opened her mouth, closed it, then opened it again. "Stuff I've never told anyone."

Her eyes welled up and Archie bit his cheek, squeezing the flesh between his teeth. He didn't have all morning to wait until Tia felt like talking. She needed to start now, to stop crying, to snap out –

"You're not like other boys, Archie Maxwell."

"Yeah, you said that under the bridge." Archie could hear the irritation in his voice, but Tia didn't seem to notice.

"In a good way. Most boys would have taken advantage. And they'd be pushing me now, to talk about it, or whatever. But you – you're patient."

Archie snorted. "Trust me, I'm not." His knee was bouncing up and down, his fingers drumming against his legs. "You don't have a bottle of water, do you?" His tongue was sandpaper, scraping the roof of his mouth.

"You're *good*," Tia went on. "And you saved me, Archie. Honestly."

"A can of Coke, or something?" he said, checking his phone once more.

09.17

The numbers changed.

09.18

That was, what? How many seconds did he have left? Nerves sent Archie to his feet and he began to pace – to and fro, to and fro – his heart pounding as he peered down the track. It swam before his eyes like a mirage, hardly real.

"For God's sake, Archie. I'm trying to tell you something! What's up with you?"

Archie almost yelled the truth but he forced himself to breathe. "It's ... nothing. Just ... Nothing. You should go, OK?" He grabbed Tia's wrist, dragging her along the embankment, back towards the bridge.

"Hey, stop it!" Tia protested. "What are you doing? You're hurting me!"

"I just don't think you should be here, all right?"

Archie said. "Not when the train goes past. It'll be too difficult."

Tia yanked her arm free. "It won't! Just listen, will you?" She rubbed her wrist, flexing her fingers. "That's what I'm trying to say. You saved me, telling me what you did about Tathum." She gave Archie a watery smile, gratitude seeping down her cheeks. "You're, like, my hero. I mean it. I'm not taking the piss."

Her perfume filled the air as she moved in close. It happened in slow motion – Tia's hand lifting, her thumb tracing the scar on Archie's cheek, her head tilting, tilting, tilting –

– and her mouth widening in shock as Archie shoved her in the chest. She slipped down the embankment, landing in a heap on the track.

"I'm not your hero!" Archie cried. "I didn't save you! Not even close!"

Confusion made a tangle of Tia's features. "I don't get it," she said. "I don't get you. What's so bad about being my –"

"Because it's a lie, OK?" Archie's words bounced off the track and startled a bird from a tree. "I made it up."

"What?"

"You heard me. You say you like the truth? Here it is. I never saw Tathum. Not once." Archie waited for Tia to reply, but she'd frozen on the track. "I'm sorry. I didn't do it to hurt you, I swear." Silence. "You were just so sad, and I thought it might help." Still nothing. "Say something, Tia. Please."

"Tathum was in love with Jared." Tia's voice was quiet, no more than a whisper.

"What did you say?"

"He liked Jared. My brother. He told me four days before he died." Tia glared at Archie. "That's why it was so important to work out when you'd seen him by the track. Two weeks before he killed himself, you said. I thought I was off the hook." She grimaced. "The night Tathum told me, he'd been drinking, maybe more than usual, I don't know. He turned off the computer in the middle of a game. I shouted at him because I was winning and he told me to shut up and listen." Tia's voice was hardly audible now. "He said he was sick of hiding it. That he wanted to come out. And I ... I told him not to." Tia's face sunk into her hands. "Can you believe that? I said it wasn't a good time. And it wasn't!" She peered at Archie from between her fingers. "Dad was drinking a lot. Mum was up to here –" She jabbed her forehead. "We fought about it, nothing major – at least, I didn't think so, you know? But then he went and –"

"Tia, I'm sorry. I really am. But it's not your fault. You get that, right?" Archie crouched in front of her. "You're not to blame."

"How do you know, Archie? You didn't see him! You lied to me. I believed you. But now –" Tia dug her fingers into her temples – "I'm back here, aren't I? Stuck with this guilt." Her nails clawed holes in her skin. "I talked him out of telling the truth. *His* truth. Mum and Dad might have accepted him, but I just made him feel ashamed. And then he jumped in front of a fucking train! How is that not my fault?"

"Listen to me," Archie said, checking the track once more. "You're right. I didn't see him. But I do know it wasn't your fault, OK? You didn't tell him to jump. You didn't push him." A flicker of movement caught Archie's attention, but it was just a tree, shedding its leaves, branches like bones under the bleak sky. "You've got to get off here, Tia. It isn't safe."

"I can't do it, Archie. Not again. I won't. *I killed him, I killed him* – round and round my head. And I can't put it right, no matter how many times I visit his grave. Give him one of those." She pointed at the red rose shining among the white flowers. "Jared. Ja-*red*. One speck of truth in all the bullshit. But it's not enough, is it? I silenced my brother. And now he doesn't have a voice at all."

Archie fumbled with his phone, his hand shaking so much he could hardly tap the screen. "The train will be here in two minutes. Stand up!" It took him three attempts to pull Tia to her feet before Archie realised she wasn't going to move.

"I'm tired, Archie. I've had enough." Tia lay down on the track, gripping the metal so hard her knuckles turned white.

"What the hell are you doing?" Archie said.

"Just go. Leave me."

Archie tried to pull away her fingers. "No, Tia. No! Don't do this! Please!"

"I've got to. It's the only way. I don't have a choice. You don't understand."

"I do, actually," Archie replied, tugging at her stubborn hands. "My dad's gay, all right?" It burst out of him, before he could stop it. "He told me on Friday. I can't handle it. I'm not handling it! My sisters, my mum, they're fine! They're cool. And I want to be too. But I'm struggling." Archie stopped trying to un-grip Tia's fingers from the track, his hand holding onto hers instead. "I'm really struggling."

Tia's eyes met Archie's. "You didn't come here for Tathum, did you?" The question was answered by the rumble of an engine. "Shit, Archie. There it is!"

The track started to vibrate, rousing the black

creature in Archie's chest. It let out a wild cry of joy. The end was here, just one last minute to endure and then everything would stop. The ache of Archie's heart. The pain in his stomach. Fifty seconds. Forty. No more Leon. No more Malcolm. No more Dad.

Dad in his old tracksuit top, cheering Archie on.

Dad wearing a head torch, peeing on a mountain.

Dad in a woolly hat, sledging over a ramp in the snow.

"Dad!" Archie shouted as the train's brakes squealed. It wasn't stopping, and they hadn't moved, and the train was going to hit. "We have a choice, Tia! We do! And I choose my dad!"

Archie pulled her again, pulled with all his might, and this time Tia let herself be saved as she yelled her brother's name. The train screeched past, inches from where they lay, panting among the flowers, the red rose between them – as fragile, as strong as a beating heart.

Three months later

"I vote pizza," Archie said. "Even you can't screw up pizza."

Dad grinned, grabbing a trolley. "I'm not giving you pizza for tea. What would Mum say? I'll make spag bol, if that suits Tia?"

Tia nodded. "Fine by me."

"I'm with Archie," Malcolm said as they stepped into the shop. "We don't want food poisoning. No offence, Tim."

"What is this?" Dad said. "I can cook!"

Archie made a face. "That stew last Saturday, Dad. The potatoes! Were they even peeled, let alone cooked?"

"Of course they were!" Behind Dad's back, Malcolm shook his head, and Archie laughed. "Fine," Dad said. "They were a tiny bit crunchy. But this'll be easier. The *spag* part anyway. The *bol* might be trickier, but

I'll give it my best shot. Right." Dad peered down an aisle. "Mince."

The temperature cooled as they walked towards the meat fridge. Archie's bare arms and legs prickled with goose bumps. His football kit was soaked, his knees were muddy, and his elbow sported a nasty graze, but it was worth it. That goal! The winner in the semi-final of the Yorkshire schools' cup! Mum and Dad had gone mad, embarrassingly so, jumping around like fools on the side line, but Archie had loved it. It hadn't been an easy few weeks. Family therapy. Personal therapy. Archie had talked more in the last three months than he had in three years. Whacking that ball had felt good.

Dad tossed two packets of mince into the trolley. "Tomatoes, next. And a red onion. Spaghetti. Beef stock?" He glanced at Malcolm.

"Beef stock," Malcom confirmed. They shared a smile, a touch. Archie looked away, looked to make sure that no one from school was around, looked to see if anyone was about to comment. But there was nothing, just people going about their everyday lives, like they were.

"Where will we find that then?" Dad asked. "Aisle ..."

"Three," came a voice behind them. Archie turned to see Leon and his mum, Pat. "Aisle three," Pat repeated. "Back that way."

"Pat!" Dad said. "Nice to see you. How are things?"

Pat answered, but Archie didn't hear it. Blood was ringing in his ears, pounding in his temples. Leon's black eyes crawled over Dad and Malcolm before settling on Archie's hot face.

"Hello, Archibald," Leon said in a low voice, as Dad and Pat chatted and Malcolm headed off in search of the beef stock. "Trust your dad to be checking out the meat. Loves a bit of pork, doesn't he?"

Tia sighed. "What's wrong with you?"

"What's wrong with Archibald, more like?" Leon asked. "Have you seen the colour of him?"

Tia slipped her hand in Archie's, but he let go, ashamed of the sweatiness of his palm, the thump of his pulse in his wrist. The graze on his elbow throbbed. He looked at the cut, expecting to see fresh blood, but no. Despite the pain, it was OK.

"Not that I blame him," Leon went on. "I wouldn't be seen dead in a place like this if it was my dad. What must everyone be thinking?"

Malcolm strolled back with the stock, dropping it in the trolley and standing next to Dad, closer than a friend would, close enough to reveal the truth, but no one paid any attention. A woman with a toddler put some chicken drumsticks in her basket. An old man was choosing between two types of beef burgers. A young couple consulted a shopping list before picking up a leg of lamb.

"Nothing," Archie said, and his voice was quiet, but calm. "They're not thinking anything, apart from what they might cook for tea tonight." This time, Archie took Tia's hand, his skin still clammy, but his pulse steady, his grip firm. "And right now all I care about is the spaghetti bolognese my dad's cooking for us and Malcolm."

"Spaghetti *bologn-aids*, more like," Leon snarled. "Wait till I tell everyone at school, Archibald."

Leon's words hovered in the air – like bees, perhaps, if Archie had chosen to feel their sting. Instead, he shrugged.

"Tell them what you like," Archie said. "But, Leon, if you call me Archibald one more time –"

"What, you'll knock me out, will you?"

"I won't, mate." Archie grinned. "But Jared will."

Dad and Malcolm said goodbye to Pat and set off to find the rest of the ingredients. Tia followed, chatting away, giggling at their jokes. Archie watched as they wandered into the dairy section, watched as they stopped to pick up some cheese ... a pint of milk ... some blueberry yoghurts for Amy. They moved in and out of the crowd, no more or less a part of it than anyone else.

Archie hurried to join them.

When life feels really hard

Archie in *The Last Days of Archie Maxwell* is
vulnerable to feeling suicidal, as are some of the other
characters. The news of his dad's sexuality, along
with the bullying that he suffers, make Archie feel
so intensely negative that he finds it hard to see the
point in carrying on.

Archie finds the courage to talk with Tia about
how he feels – and about how she feels too – but
mental illness is something many people find very
difficult to talk about.

If you are struggling with how you feel and need
to talk to someone, you can call these free helplines.
They offer comfort, advice and protection to children
and young people.

Childline (UK)
0800 1111

Samaritans (UK)
116 123

Are you a book eater or a book avoider – or something in between?

This book is designed to help more people love reading. Tender and spirited, *The Last Days of Archie Maxwell* tells of the destructive nature of secrets and their amazing power to heal, if shared. It thrums with courage, compassion and wit – it's a heart-stopper of a story by a uniquely brilliant author. There is plenty here for book lovers to treasure. At the same time, it has clever design features to support more readers.

You may notice the book is printed on heavy paper in two colours – black for the text and a pale yellow Pantone® for the page background. This reduces the contrast between text and paper and hides the 'ghost' of the words printed on the other side of the page. For readers who perceive blur or movement as they read, this may help keep the text still and clear. The book also uses a unique typeface that is dyslexia-friendly.

If you're a book lover, and you want to help spread the love, try recommending *The Last Days of Archie Maxwell* to someone you know who doesn't like books. You never know – maybe a super-readable book is all they need to spark a lifelong love of reading.